Grit

New stories

by Yorkshire Writers

Nettle Books

Published 2017 by Nettle Books, Yorkshire

nettlebooks@hotmail.co.uk

Stories © 2017 by the authors

This collection © 2017 by Nettle Books

ISBN: 978-0-9933729-3-3

Classification: Fiction

Foreword: When grit means pluck and passion

Ian Clayton

Grit. I like the sound of that word. It signals backbone, pluck, perhaps passion.

The famous opening passage in Barry Hines's book *A Kestrel for a Knave* contains that word.

"There were no curtains up. Inside the bedroom, the darkness was of a gritty texture."

It *feels* like a northern word, it probably *is* a northern word.

To do with hardness, wuthering and stuff blowing into your eye.

This book collects together stories by Yorkshire writers.

The stories are not all set in Yorkshire: *A Stolen Night* is a story of sex on a beach in India.

When Fat Ruled the World comes from a non-place-specific dystopian future where obese goddesses are wheeled on to the stage for judgement.

While *Rudolf Gets a Grandma* seems to come from a future nearby and is a quirky fantasy about how we treat the older generation.

Michael Yates, who put this anthology together, tells me that he drew mainly from writers' workshops in Wakefield and Pontefract.

The invitation was to write a short story of no more than 5,000 words and there was no theme.

When you read these stories, my guess is that you will create your own patterns.

It's a bit like making your way down a path made from crazy paving, each piece with its own tale to tell, but also fitting where perhaps it's not supposed to, to tell a bigger story.

So, we get twilight worlds, rites of passage and longing. *Still Life with Fruit* is a good example of this longing. A grandfather looks forward to his granddaughter's journey into the future while remembering where the journey started.

And in *Points of Convergence* we are drawn into an inspired imagining about the 1960's and a past that never really goes away.

I like to find stuff, wind-blown messages, washed-up pieces of wood, stones with an unusual shape.

Sometimes your eye falls on things that you wouldn't ordinarily see, at other times these things blow right into your eye.

That's the nub of this book I guess: what you might call coming right down to the real nitty-gritty.

Ian Clayton, Featherstone, 2017

*Dedicated to Yorkshire writer
the late Howard Frost,
much respected and missed by his
contemporaries*

Contents

Minor Problem

Joan Thornton

I WAS DOING MY BEST to persuade Mum to let me shorten my school skirt. Knowing how keen she was about money-saving or time-saving tips, I went for the economic argument: fabric content of miniskirts compared with calf length, saving on washing powder, ironing and electricity – and time. She looked at me thoughtfully for a moment. I imagined I'd convinced her but then she shook her head in exasperation.

"If I didn't know we're only related by marriage, I'd swear you inherited your gormlessness from Ann Tett."

I was devastated by the comparison. Uncle Gilbert and Ann Tett lived in the next village and she was the loopy front runner, way ahead of all the other family oddballs. But we'd been to visit only two days before so no doubt the memory still rankled.

"Saaandraaaa, Saaandraaaa!" screeched the mynah bird.

"Saaandraaaa, Saaandraaaa!" screeched Ann Tett in perfect imitation.

"Saaandraaaa, Saaandraaaa!" responded the mynah bird.

"Saaandraaaa, Saaandraaaa!" screeched Ann Tett.

"God Almighty! Shut that racket!" roared Uncle Gilbert over the noise of the mynah bird's follow-up. It effectively shut up the mynah bird but not Ann Tett.

"Don't shout at her!" yelled Ann Tett, "You'll upset her. Saaandraaaa, Saaandraaaa!" she coaxed.

Uncle Gilbert stomped out of the kitchen and slammed the door.

"Gone up allotment," she said indifferently.

It seemed to have a mollifying effect on the mynah bird which cocked its head on one side, eyed the door with its bright coal-black eyes and screeched "Saaandraaaa!" as if determined to have the last word. The raucous sound filled the tiny living-kitchen and Ann Tett's response was like a conditioned reflex.

It was both fascinating and repulsive the way her lips puckered around her toothless mouth and flapped loosely when she talked. Her cheeks sucked in and out like bellows; but when she shrieked at the bird, her lips stretched into a wide pink rim exposing her orange gums and yellow furred tongue. It was difficult to hide my revulsion.

I knew Ann Tett had teeth but I'd never seen her with them in. She used to keep them in a pretty china mug on the kitchen windowsill. I'd once picked it up to have a drink of water. I filled it from the tap and brought it to my lips before seeing the pink and white dentures grinning at me. Shocked, I threw it into the sink and the china mug smashed, leaving the teeth circling the plughole like a vampire coming up the drain.

Ann Tett cackled at my panic like one of Macbeth's old witches. Mum nattered about my clumsiness as she carefully picked the teeth out of the sink because I couldn't bring myself to touch them. She dropped them into a jam jar, topped them up with water and put them back on the windowsill where, to my knowledge, they've been ever since.

"Gilbert got the bird for me," Ann Tett told us. "He said it would be company for me when he's out, but now says he doesn't like it. Says it's noisy and he don't like the feathers and mess it makes. But it's too late now, he should have thought about that before he got it for me."

She poked her knobbly finger into the cage and addressed the bird: "I said *He should have thought about that before he got you, shouldn't he, Sandra? I said: Shouldn't he, Sandra?*"

"Saaandraaaa, Saaandraaaa!" screeched the mynah bird.

"Does it say anything else?" Mum asked quickly before the whole routine started up again.

"No," said Ann Tett, aggrieved.

"Who's Sandra?" asked my little brother Jimmy who'd just come in from the garden where he'd been throwing stones at next door's rabbit hutch.

"Dunno. That's what it said when your Uncle Gilbert got it. It's maybe the lass of the feller he got it from."

"Why don't you try saying something different to it, Ann Tett?" I suggested, "Then it might learn some new words."

She pondered this idea. Her thinking processes were sluggish. Her face had none of the bright alertness of the mynah bird, but she slowly came to a decision. "Happen I might."

I smirked behind my hand, Jimmy sniggered and nudged me hard with his elbow. I stumbled against the Aga and got coal dust on the sleeve of my blouse. I rubbed it furiously. Jimmy sniggered some more and Mum glared at us both.

"Would you like that, Sandra?"

"Saaandraaaa!" screeched the mynah bird.

"Saaandraaaa!" screeched Ann Tett.

"Saaandraaaa!" mocked Jimmy.

"For God's sake shut up!" yelled Mum, thankful at last to have somebody she could vent her irritation on.

It went quiet again. Both Ann Tett and the mynah bird looked chastened but Jimmy just smirked, which annoyed Mum all the more.

"Get outside and give us some peace," ordered Mum.

"There's nothing to do," moaned Jimmy, wanting to torment the mynah bird some more.

9

"You'll find something," said Mum, putting the kettle back on the hob. "Go see you what your Uncle Gilbert's doing up on the allotment."

I cleared off into the back garden and pulled a few weeds out of the gravel till Jimmy disappeared in the direction of the allotments and I could quietly slip back into the house and listen.

Poor Ann Tett, she couldn't help being strange. She always seemed odd, not really part of the family. Mind you, I did not actually realise that she was my aunt until I was nearly ten and I felt a real idiot when it came to light.

I was looking through a shoebox of old family photos. There was a picture of a wedding group with a very young Uncle Gilbert standing next to a very pretty, slender young woman in a long wedding dress. There was no mistaking Uncle Gilbert even in his youth. He's got the family nose and chin which don't improve with age, just become less exaggerated as obesity softens the edges of once sharp features.

"Who's that next to Uncle Gilbert?" I asked, holding up the photo.

"That's your Auntie Doreen."

Confused, I tried to figure it out for myself. "Was that before she married Uncle Bill?" I asked.

"Your Auntie Doreen and Uncle Bill got married the year before."

"Well, how come she married Uncle Gilbert if she was already married to Uncle Bill?" I asked, wondering if I'd unearthed some scandal in the family. Mum said nothing but looked at me intently, probably working out some evasive answer to cover up this skeleton in the cupboard.

"What are you on about?" She put down the iron and came and looked over my shoulder to see more clearly who I was pointing at. "You daft little beggar, *that's* your Auntie Doreen on the other side. That..." she said, pointing at the bride, "is Ann Tett. Not the sharpest knife in the drawer even then, but no doubting that she was a real bonny lass."

What a revelation! Ann Tett had once been very pretty. Beautiful, in fact. But then the confusion became worse.

"You mean Ann Tett is really Auntie Ann?"

Mum also looked confused. "No. Ann Tett."

"That's what I said. *Ann*," I paused, "*Tett*."

"Not Ann Tett – *Aunt Ett*." Mum stressed the Aun…T and E…tt.

I was stunned. You see, Mum always used to say: "We'll go visit Uncle Gilbert and Ann Tett." Or "Uncle Gilbert and Ann Tett are coming over."

So far as I was concerned, Uncle Gilbert was Mum's brother and Ann Tett lived with him – probably as his housekeeper. That's what they called women who lived with men out of wedlock. It had never struck me as odd that she was always referred to by both Christian and surname. There's a lot of Anns about – it's a popular name. There were two Anns in my class so you always had to specify which you meant if you were referring to one of them. And then Ann Corbisher was one of Mum's friends and Anne Finch lived next door but one, so calling Ann Tett by both names made perfect sense.

So. Ann Tett was married to Uncle Gilbert and was really my aunt, and her name was not Ann Tett but Henrietta – Henrietta Piggot before she married Uncle Gilbert. If she had been called *Auntie* Ett, the mistake would never have happened.

I tried to make Mum see there was logic in my misunderstanding but she just started laughing, and went on laughing and laughed so hard she knocked the iron off the ironing board. That stopped her laughing. She picked up the iron and strands of molten loop-pile carpet, stretched like chewing gum, leaving a wodge of brown gunge stuck to the

11

bottom of the iron and a distinctive iron-shaped mark in the carpet. The iron ticked as it cooled, the red eye of the power indicator ominously dull. All was not well within. Mum shook it vigorously and looked at the carpet in dismay. "Oh bugger, bugger, bugger!"

It took a lot to make Mum swear. She was obviously upset by the devastation. I didn't care; I considered it retribution for her mockery. Of course she had to go tell Dad all about my stupid mistake when she was explaining the disaster. Dad just smiled grimly, looking at the carpet, poking inside the iron with a screwdriver and thinking about the cost. But the rest of the relatives found it funny when she told them.

After that, I gave serious thought to calling Ann Tett *Auntie Ett, Auntie Ettie, Aunt Henrietta* – but decided against it, knowing that I would never be able to think of her as anything other than Ann Tett. And, after all the amusement had died down, changing her name might serve to keep reminding them of my little error.

Funny how Ann Tett is our only aunt, the rest are all aunties. Maybe it has to do with the rhythm of the name. But no. It's not Aunt Amy, it's Auntie Amy. So perhaps… way back… when these things are first decided upon, it was a quiet signal that she stood apart from ordinary aunties, separated by the oddness which was apparent long before she ever had her stroke.

"How's Debbie and Colin and the kiddies?" asked Mum when we recently visited.

"Okay. Don't see much of 'em."

"How's Marlene and Harry? Is little Kate walking yet?"

"Yeh, but she's too fat."

"She'll soon get rid of it once she's walking."

"No," said Ann Tett, "our Marlene never walks anywhere."

12

"And Jeanette and *her* brood?"

"Alright I suppose." She shrugged.

"What about Fred and Lynn then? Do you see much of them and the kids?"

"They come sometimes. They're always busy... and you can't expect it of lads the same. But they're all too busy. That's why Gilbert got me the mynah bird." Unfortunately it served to remind her. "Saaandraaaa!" she shrieked at it.

Mum closed her eyes and put on her God-give-me-strength expression. I made sure only my eyes showed above the top of my book so she wouldn't see the grin on my face.

The mynah bird had been dozing on its perch but it now opened its eyes and responded like a dutiful dog. "Saaandraaaa, Saaandraaaa!" Then it retracted its head into its body and settled down again to await its next curtain call.

I reflected awhile, then decided that this appalling neglect by Ann Tett's three daughters and son was exceedingly shocking. None of them lived more than a mile away. Some of their kids even went to the local infant school which is only at the bottom of Ann Tett's road and turn left.

I could also see that Mum was very disapproving. "Can you take your nose out of that book for a minute and put the kettle on?" she said sharply.

I got the impression I was expected to listen to this bit of conversation and learn an essential lesson. Daughters are expected to demonstrate a filial devotion that is rarely demanded of sons and certainly can't be expected of daughters-in-law. Well, I know that already – my older brother Barry isn't expected to come on these dutiful visits any more, and even though I'm also old enough to stay on my own, I don't get out of it, not even by pleading I've got piles of homework to do. I've heard it all before. Mothers have to just count themselves lucky if their sons drop on a decent lass who fits in with the family and knows her responsibilities. But daughters have duties as well as responsibilities. Duties to take care of old parents and grandparents and anybody else that needs anything doing for them.

"The trouble is that Ann Tett's daughters are all flibberty-gibbets, and their mother sets them no example if naming all your children after film stars is any measure of good sense," says Auntie Amy. Frequently.

Flibberty-gibbet! Such a splendid expression. I've only ever known Jane Austen, Julie Andrews and Auntie Amy ever use it. I wondered where she picked that up because she never reads novels and I doubt she's ever seen *The Sound of Music* because she doesn't hold with entertainment mocking God. By that, I presume, she means the singing nuns.

"Pleasure for the sake of pleasure destroys the brain cells." Not sure where she got that one from either; maybe she was confusing it with masturbation. But I suppose it amounts to the same thing.

Mind you, Ann Tett's flibberty-gibbet daughters are a lot more interesting than the decent, responsible lasses who've overrun our family.

Sometimes *I'm* torn between being a decent lass and a flibberty-gibbet. On balance, I'd choose flibberty-gibbet, but I'm not sure I could cope with Mum's disapproval. They do seem to have a lot more fun though. They laugh a lot more, loud infectious laughter, not little titters and simpers. We don't see much of them though. Christmas and other family events – and, of course, when Ann Tett had her stroke and everybody thought she would die.

For three days everybody was packed in the hospital corridor, waiting their turn to go in two by two. Then, when the doctor said that Ann Tett was out of danger, the rush slowed to a trickle in danger of drying up. So Auntie Amy dutifully organised a rota to make sure that everybody was doing their fair share of visiting and taking responsibility.

When I was younger, Ann Tett's peculiar ways fascinated me. "What's that?" I might ask.

"Shim-shams for meddlers," was her inevitable reply followed by an insane cackle of laughter as if she'd just delivered a startling piece of wit.

It took me some time to figure out that she either didn't know the answer or was telling me to mind my own business. Then, after Ann Tett's stroke, which affected her speech and what it did to her brain is anybody's guess, her cackling "shim-shams for meddlers" was her answer to most things.

As I got older, her novelty value wore thin and I started to find her stupidity irritating.

"Which school did you go to?" I once asked her. Having just passed my eleven plus for grammar school, education was a subject of great interest to me.

"I went to Miss Primm's school of Ard-Knox." That's how the name appeared in my mind's eye.

I was surprised but impressed by the idea of her going to some posh private school. She seemed to have come out of it pretty ignorant, but I knew that finishing schools are less concerned with education than making girls marriageable. Stories about boarding schools featured heavily on my reading list at that time. So when I tried to elicit more information about this special school, my misunderstanding became apparent. She thought it was a huge joke and cackled hysterically till she started choking.

Mum made me get some water while she thumped on her back. I debated briefly about giving her the jar of water with the dentures in. I listened to the sound of her wheezing whoops as she gasped for breath and I slowly washed a dusty glass while she died.

"Get a move one on," shouted Mum. So I did and she recovered.

We left to get the five past bus. The bus stop was only about ten yards from the back door but because of the angle of the house, you couldn't see the bus approaching. Normally, when it's time to leave, Mum transfers to a chair by the kitchen door with her coat and bag and sends one of us to keep a lookout and give her a shout when the bus comes into sight. If nobody's waiting at the bus stop and nobody wants to get off the bus, the driver zooms past without stopping. On this occasion however, long before the bus was due, we all stood at the bus stop to wait. I think she'd found Ann Tett and the mynah bird more wearing than usual.

Jimmy moseyed up the back garden and, from the clunking sounds, I suspected he was lobbing stones at the rabbit hutch again. I propped myself against the bus stop and read my book. Mum kept looking at her watch in exasperation as if the bus was running late, then she'd turn and wave to Ann Tett, who'd heaved herself to the window and was forlornly watching our departure.

"Are you off then?" Uncle Gilbert shambled over, smelling of warm bran mash and pig muck.

"Aye, we'd better be off. I want to get Ted's dinner on – he's on afters."

"And I'd better get myself cleaned up and see to Ett – I'm on nights."

"Don't the lasses come over and see she's alright while you're at work?" Mum asked ....rather craftily, I thought.

"No. But we manage. That's why I got her that bloody bird, for a bit of company when she's on her own, to try and make up for the girls not visiting her very often. The grand-kiddies are her only real pleasure and she hardly sees anything of them."

I wondered if Ann Tett got her pleasure out of mocking and humiliating them as much as she did me.

"Trouble is," went on Uncle Gilbert, "them husbands of theirs are all shiftless. Maybe Colin's not quite as shiftless as the other two, he does work from time to time. But shiftless

16

is still shiftless, and the lasses..." He shook his head in dismay.

Uncle Gilbert's soul-baring was a wonderful eye-opener; he'd never been a great conversationalist. From the corner of my eye I saw him glance in my direction. I kept my eyes riveted on my book with what I hoped was a look of intense concentration. It must have looked convincing enough.

"And the lasses?" Mum prompted gently.

"Well, the lasses... trouble is they take too much after their mother – a bit flighty and no money sense at all."

Fabulous. Shiftless husbands and flighty flibberty-gibbet wives. What a combination. However, in the light of this information, I decided I should seriously reconsider any ambitions to be a flibberty-gibbet if it meant marrying a shiftless man.

"Always on the cadge. Never get from one rent day to the next without one or other of them coming round to borrow money. Maybe they work it out between them because they do seem to do it in turn. Always promise to pay it back of course. Full of promises they are."

"Well, why do you keep giving it to them?" asked Mum.

"But what else can I do? I think of the grand-kiddies. You can't see them kiddies without a roof over their heads or food on the table. Because they're always famished when they *do* come to visit. I can see our Marlene's pair get through a whole loaf of bread-and-jam sandwiches when they come. I just can't bear to see them kids go without so..."

"No, you can't," said Mum sympathetically.

"And then what happens? A week goes by and they say they'll pay me back the week after. And the week after, they don't come round at all. It can then go for weeks without them bringing the grand-kiddies round and it breaks Ett's heart not to see them. So in the end I have to go round to their house and say: *forget about the money, you don't need to pay me back, just bring the bairns round to visit your mother, she misses them a lot.* So they start coming round again and for a few weeks everything's alright till it starts all over again. *Dad, rent's overdue. We're three weeks behind. Can you lend us some money? And this time I promise I'll pay you back.* And so I keep on paying. Because that's how I see it, paying my kids to come and visit their own mother so she can see her own grandchildren.

"Ett spends half her time weeping over them and there's nothing to be gained by me saying *They're your kids, they take after you and you've made them as they are.* What's done is done. But it's true, when they were little she spoiled them rotten. Never said no to anything they wanted. Always let them have their own way. No discipline. And I was never there to say anything. I was always at work to earn the overtime to pay for everything. So maybe I should take some of the blame on myself. I should have been at home more to see that they got a bit of discipline."

Oh wow, this was great. It was the longest speech I'd ever heard him make. And he hadn't finished.

"After all, I can't say I don't know what Ett's like. She's always been a bit of a handful herself…"

At that, Uncle Gilbert tailed off but I saw his half-smile as he turned his head and winked at Ann Tett still standing at the window. It was that wink, more than anything else which convinced me that the pretty but now unrecognisable bride in the wedding photo really was Ann Tett.

Mum also saw the wink and her lips tightened in disapproval. "You always were too easily taken in by a pretty face and now look where it's got you."

"Anyway," he said with resignation, "here's your bus and I'd better go get myself ready for work."

18

"You'll be working till you drop to keep them lasses of yours and their shiftless husbands," said Mum.

It was a sad little tale, but Uncle Gilbert just shrugged.

"Saaandraaaa, Saaandraaaa!" came the raucous screech from the open doorway.

"Saaandraaaa, Saaandraaaa!"

We listened to the answering call, not knowing which was Ann Tett and which was the mynah bird.

Uncle Gilbert smiled grimly. "Maybe I will. Maybe I will. But I'll make sure that bloody bird goes before I do."

An Ever So Small Step Too Far

Neil Fieldhouse

FIRST, LET ME SAY, AND THIS IS DIFFICULT, because I am shaking, shaking so badly I have to clench my entire body, my teeth, to try to keep some control and that's the fear, not the cold, but what I want to say and I will, I will now say is this: *I am not a monster.*

No-one would suggest I am.

In fact, let me make absolutely clear, no question: *I am not a monster.* No-one would point, say: *There's a monster.* I would shout, if I could: *I am not a monster.* But I can hardly speak at all because of this tightness gripping me. At least, I don't think I can. But did I? Did I just shout: *I am not a monster?* I may have.

I stand here, right now, at this moment, on the very edge, a rope around my bare neck – it's only my neck that's bare, I am washed and shaved and dressed, the usual blue jeans and a rather dull grey shirt, I'd like to say *dove* grey because that would suggest softness and peace, but that's hardly how it is – tight, scratching. I don't know what is out there, in front. A void. Is it? No-one has pulled a hood down low. I can see – but there's nothing in front, nothing I can focus on. A blur through my tears and fingers. There's a breeze, a light breeze, a cool, light breeze murmuring in my face. I don't wear a hood. Not yet. And yes, my fingers are across my eyes so my hands are free. I am not shackled, not yet, though I cannot reach out, they are frozen where they are. I have them clasped across my face. I would try to loosen the choking rope, but....

And all the time, my legs, my legs, they are mine, my whole body is shaking, trembling.

I cannot stop it. I'm sorry, I can't. Violent shakes. Convulsions. People are saying: *he's having fits, having the shits*. They are saying, they are looking and laughing: *he's like a drunk, a stupid drunk*. He's bloody scared. Coward. And I am.

I feel nothing under me, my feet numb, knees knocking, feel nothing firm beneath me. Is this wood under my feet? I dare not, cannot stamp to find out. Cannot shift my feet, not a shuffle. Dare not shift. It could give way any moment. *Whoooooosh*. Gone. My whole world about to open beneath me. My life drop far, far down.

The breeze is now a little stronger, chattering now. A little cooler and I'm finding it difficult to stand straight. It's the convulsions, the dragging knot in my stomach. I'm doubling up. But as my body bends, the rope tightens. Burns. I cannot move my hands to ease it. I dare not. There will be people. There *are* people. People out there. Out there. They can see me. In front. Staring. Wishing what of me? Thinking what of me? Hating me. Why would they hate me? I am not guilty. I have done nothing to them. I have made clear: *I am no monster*. Let me spell that out: *I am not a monster*. I am also not a fool here with my hands covering my eyes, I am not thinking: *If I can't see them, then they can't see me*. Oh no. I just dare not look.

Tears and snot are on my fingers. I am crying, I admit that, but not because I am sorry for myself. Oh no. I feel no self-pity, standing here, rope around my neck. I got over that a long time ago. I just feel fear, a deep, deep, body-torturing fear. I would defy anyone not to cry, given my position.

I am not a monster. I have said that. But I suppose, I suppose I have to admit that, yes, okay, yes, I have killed. My wife? She had hopes, she had dreams. They are gone. It could have been our children too, but I never got that far. Not my own. That never happened. I tell you now: *It did not happen*. Shall I spell that out? Shall I?

21

This morning, because this is morning, a spring day, the gate open. Open wide. It is a gate, not a door, not a door of steel. It is a gate. That hard knotting in my stomach is now a piercing pain. A lance. *Agggh,* a bullet. Blue paint flaking on the gate, the number *16* in white plastic. That's how I see it, with a garden beyond as you approach from the pavement. I do remember gardens.

I think, now I think about it, that's why I've come to this. This moment now, here, where I am now. The love of the garden. It's the scent... the sweet, deep scent of, of, of lupins. Wow, yes, I can see them now, and as I think of them, the iron bands gripping me begin to relax. I see them sturdy on the edge of the border, waist high, tall spikes of strawberry, chocolate – not the shitty brown stuff, no, no, that creamy white chocolate, and raspberry and blueberry and candy floss pink. This is how I think of colours, as flavours, so I can smell them, taste them, get the fullness of them. And a tower of sweet peas, the first of the season to open, fresh this morning. Their heavy scent takes me to my mother, all those years ago.

If she saw me now, she'd be so ashamed. So would my father. Disgusted at what I am. Their son. What I've become. But they are long dead – not by my hand, please, let me emphasise that. I did not.

A sun, a buttery sun. You see, I can taste and smell the sun. It's there, in my mind, in my garden. And a tree, a giant oak tree, its damp bark liquorice black and leaves the sharp colour of lemon and limes. There has been a shower of rain, silver rain, warm, and the smell of the grass. Unmistakable. Have you even been in a desert, yearned for that smell of fresh cut grass?

Each day I hear the blue gate squeal open, squeal closed. Shut. Every day because I am never anywhere else. I must oil it. Can I? No, I don't mean I am always here, right here, not just here, on this spot, right where I am now, no, no, no. I am always just behind here, somewhere just behind where I am now, I cannot look round, cannot turn, where I stand, well, crouch now, because the pain is so bad, the cramp so deep, so crippling I am doubling up. It hurts so deep down. Thankfully, they have allowed the rope to sag, but they'll tighten it again. Oh yes. They must be making adjustments behind me, fiddling with knots, pulleys. I don't know how it works. I cannot see. But they'll pull me upright. Violently.

There are voices. A low murmuring and it could be them. Or is it the breeze? People talk about the wind, but they should talk about the noise of the wind. Listen to it. Do it in the future, because I won't. Listen to the wind. Or is it the people now gathered in front? Are they the ones? Is it their mocking chatter? I manage to keep my hands over my eyes. The shame. The shame.

The rope sags. Thank God, because I'm almost flat out, foetal like. He's a bastard. Who? God. Don't be shocked. What else do you expect of me? If you were here. If I were you – is that right? If you were me – is that right? Whatever, no matter, God-the-bastard, it hurts. Let me tell you now, you'd think just the same. Perhaps worse. And oh, so holy, you are saying to yourself: that could never be me. Me? I would never. Really?

I shake even more now. I am getting angry. I have to count back from ten. Slowly. Down to one. But what is the point? Each a second of life away, wasted, where there is so little left. So very little.

But I am a little calmer now.

I ease open, widen the gap between my middle and my ring finger, I think those are they, the middle and the ring, over my right eye. My vision is very blurred. I blink. There's a film of goo over my eye. I will not, I cannot, shift and I cannot focus.

Slowly, because I don't want sudden movement, not with this rope at my neck, even though it's still slack it could jerk tight at any time, but slowly I take my hand away, my right one. I close my eye against the buttery sun. I take my hand away and ever so slowly, from where I now lie, curled and rigid, I try to reach behind, to touch whatever is there. I expect voices shouting: *Stop*. But, no. So I continue, reaching far behind, careful because I can feel my arm unbalancing me, threatening to roll me over. On my back. And then I would be vulnerable. Behind. Nothing. Nothing? How can this be?

I am never anywhere else but just behind me, in that room. Where has it gone? Footsteps are running towards me. I cannot look. I curl further into a ball. Adrenaline now pushing the pain away.

The day started as all my days do. In this cell of mine. It *is* a cell. Let's not call it anything else. Oh, I have comforts, a television, radio. I cannot figure computers, though there is one. I am fed. Meals are regular, but I don't taste them, I have no sense of taste, not now. These senses – taste, smell – they exist only in my memory. I suppose they have gone because they aren't needed here. Touch, yes. Sight, yes. Hearing, yes. Taste, no. Smell, no. I think I once read that the two are related – smell, the stink of things, that's the keenest and it's gone, and taste has gone with it. Is fear a sense? I have that. I know, I know. I am not a fool.

There's a comfortable bed, an oh-so-comfortable bed. And the warmth of someone beside me.

I can manage everything else. No-one needs to knock on the door. No-one needs to ask me to open up. I wouldn't. Couldn't. There's a bin outside. Leave it there.

When I am in there, that room behind me, somewhere behind me because, and I can feel the panic and fear rising, because I cannot tell where it is. My hand, my right arm, is now reaching as far as I can. Nothing. But when I am in there, then I am fine. Secure, warm. Out there, well, not there, because this is where I am now, out, so I suppose it's out *here*. Well, out here is some place I did not need to think about, ever. Well, I *couldn't* think about. My whole self would begin to close down as an avalanche of horror poured into me. I can use words. I am no fool. Well, I say I am no fool, yet I did not anticipate that this day would come. A sort of day of reckoning. And that is my fault. All my fault. I should have known. Should have planned. Should have ignored the banging on the wall.

In truth, there have been moments in the past, moments when I began to think I would be where I now am. On the outside. But those are not thoughts to dwell on. And, like I say, they are not thoughts that get far in me before my own defences rush to close them down. But, let me say again, there was this banging on the wall. And then I heard the voice. *Hers.* I know her voice. Sometimes she visits. There are visitors and I am glad to see them. And, yes, I admit, sometimes when they leave, I would like to be able to follow them. Outside. She is slightly younger than me. Everyone seems to be. I feel so, so old. What, in her thirties, I would hazards a guess. Tall, slim, well, normally slim, with intense blue eyes. I expected black hair because I know her parents are Irish, but she's fair. And there you are, sometimes the unexpected. And I digress. In fact, I feel calmer. If this is my fate, then this is my fate.

Her name? Oh God-the-bastard, I cannot remember, oh yes, yes. Helen. She visited a few days ago, heavily pregnant, which is a joy, I am told. She wanted advice. Would it hurt? I howled with laughter. Hurt? Wow. I began to answer, but I was ignored. Tea was poured and I rose from my chair and drifted from the room.

And then this morning. As usual. The radio on, BBC Radio 2, I don't like it too loud. I am scoring well on the Ken Bruce pop music quiz. The banging starts. On the wall. So loud. And then Helen screaming, screaming for my wife, for Susan, who is of course at work, and then for me. Me? Is she crazy?

25

Our walls are not thin. You cannot hear everything, but someone screaming like that, like blue murder, well, you could hear her on the other side of the world. She must be panicking because she calls my name, even though she knows. She knows.

"Please help me! John! John! Help!" Bang. Bang. "Help!"

I know what's wrong. The baby. She has no telephone next door. The place is divided into three flats. We never have trouble from them. A single mum-to-be. Hard up. She comes to our house. Uses ours. Her mobile presumably lost. Again. You see, I'm rational. No problem. My breathing is getting sharper. Building to something? I don't know. I do feel calmer now. Talking about this. I'm bringing my arm back from behind. It's terrifying me because I can't feel anything there. So I'll curl here. Just curl up. Wait for them to pull. Like a dog on a lead. A dog.

That banging. "John!" A terrible scream. "John, help me! Coming!" I panic. I should go to the phone and call an ambulance. But, well, I don't know, I just don't. I don't. Do I want to be a hero? No. No. I'm just not thinking. Not straight.

I go to our door. The front door. The door leading directly outside. And I freeze there. But that screaming. Is she dying? I lean towards the wall. Can almost hear her breathing. I have been through this door a thousand times and more, but this door, it's not locked, oh no, but this door I haven't opened for such a long, long time. In my mind I have it as a garden gate, with the garden beyond. I can cope with that. I don't see the solid wooden, brown front door. I see the gate now, peeling blue, and the garden beyond, so perhaps, perhaps, that's why I think about opening it.

Anything for the smell of lupins.

Screaming and banging.

I reach down to the handle, a curved brass handle. Cold and very, very smooth. And I push down on it, feeling the springs tense, its inner workings grating, the latch scraping back and the door slowly giving.

Those screams.

I step back, pulling slightly at the door, a little resistance seems to ask "am I sure?" and it gives, moves so freely. That slight squeak of the hinges. Step back again as it opens. The light. And I stand staring out into the void beyond. I grip the door, anchor myself, but the screaming.

The screaming. No name now, just the horrible, horrible screams.

One step forward, carpet beneath me, and then another, longer, more a stride, over the wooden threshold and one foot onto the edge of the wide, stone front step. The breeze. I cling to the handle, slowly reach round with my left hand to grip the outside handle, and then ease my body out onto that step. My weight shifts and suddenly I stumble a little, my hand twists from the handle.

Oh, that screaming.

I can hardly balance. I teeter on that front step. Hands free. Wavering.

The screaming.

I can't go on. Not out here. I reach back for the door. And then, then, a gust of wind, it must be that, it slams behind me. Oh my God-the-bastard! Then the rope tightens at my neck. There is nowhere to go. Neither backwards nor forwards.

And now those voices. They are coming. "Get back!"

SUSAN WOOD turns her Mini sharp right, no indicators, no pause, blind to other traffic, into the street where she lives. Park View. A long row of Edwardian terraced houses on one side. Low stone walls that would have been topped with iron railings had they not been sawn off years ago for the war effort. Moderate length gardens straight up to the front doors. Opposite a park. She pulls down the car's visor against the spring sunshine that slants down the road. Half way along, a police car, an ambulance. Blue lights.

Police had telephoned her at work – how she hates that job, but she has to stick with it. A neighbour had given her number. Five minutes from desk to home, if that, the school rush-hour long gone. She parks behind the police car, engine stalls, car jumps, and she sees an officer approaching. A man, was it? They all looked the same. She can't make out in the glare of the sun. She climbs out, shields her eyes.

"Mrs Wood?" It's a man.

"Yes. What on earth?"

"Your husband, I believe he's your husband, is on the front step screaming at us to keep away. I think he thinks we're going to hang him."

"You don't need the ambulance." They hurry side by side to her house.

"It's for the lady next door. Her baby, but we've another on the way."

"You don't need an ambulance. He's fine."

"He doesn't seem it."

"He has severe agoraphobia. It gives him panic attacks. If you could just help me get him back in the house, he'll be, well, he'll be okay."

A handful of people move aside and she pushes open the garden gate, hurries half-crouched up the red-tiled path towards the figure curled on the front doorstep.

"Oh, John. Please, John, it's me. Sue. I'll get you back inside." Tears drip from her cheeks as she bends, one knee on the red tiles, and puts her hand to the side of his face. "It's me." She brushes his hair to one side.

The policeman is just behind. "I think we probably ought to…"

"Please. If we can just get him back inside. Please." She slides her hand from cheek to shoulder. "John, it's me,

28

Sue. Come on," She reaches for his arm. "Please. You're safe now."

She looks up at the policeman. "If you could just help me get him up. Standing." She tugs and the figure on the stone step begins to unwind. A big, powerful looking man. The policeman steps sharply back. Begins to draw what looks like a gun.

"Don't you dare to be afraid of him. Don't you dare. He needs your help. Please, just take his arm." She reaches up to the door handle and pushes open the door. "Please help."

The policeman pauses, cautiously puts the taser gun back into its holster, takes the spare arm and the threesome step awkwardly through the door and into the front room. As the policeman squeezes through, he catches a framed picture on the wall, sends it lopsided, the uniformed soldier now smiling up at the ceiling and the medals beneath tilted towards the floor.

"Sorry."

"It's not a problem. If you could help me put him in that chair there. What was he doing outside? John, what happened?"

Ken Bruce softly introduces Olly Murs singing *Dance With Me Tonight*. Catchy rhythm, catchy. The policeman steps away, crosses the room to the door and rights the frame on the wall. Reads the caption: *Sgt John Wood, VC, 2nd Battalion Parachute Regiment, Helmand, Afghanistan*. And in bright red lipstick across the top: *My hero x*.

Rudolf Gets a Grandma

Diane Galloway

RUDOLF SWEET WAS AN ORPHAN, had spent his early life in a children's home, where the matron had named him Rudolf after a hankering for a certain Russian ballet dancer. His surname came later, derived from his sweet disposition which belied his abandonment in a dustbin as a newborn baby.

The young Rudolf did well, excelled as a scholar and, at the age of 35, had a promising career in banking. He never forgot his roots and every Christmas sent a generous cheque to the children's home that had nurtured him.

One night, feeling lonely and bored and flicking through TV channels, he happened to tune into a film called *Cocoon* which had a cast of sweet and gentle old age pensioners. He was suddenly overcome with a yearning for a grandma. The yearning was a physical ache that made his brown eyes water.

So, on a spring morning in May, he drove to an old folk's home on the outskirts of Leeds. It was a dank, dark place at the bottom of a long gravel drive, Gothic in appearance with grey spires and ugly grotesques. Iron bars striped the small mullioned windows. Someone with a sense of humour had hung a vest behind one of them with the word HELP scrawled between the armholes. There were two entrances, one marked *Grandmas*, the other *Granddads*. On both sides of the drive were tall trees and, high in their budding branches, were huddles of skulking black crows flapping like discarded bin bags, their brittle caws rending the softness of the day.

A woman in a blue tabard was standing outside the *Grandmas* entrance drawing on a cigarette. She was biker-boot-deep in cigarette butts. Rudolf slid out of the driving seat and walked up to her with his easy masculine grace. She appraised him through squinting eyes, the creased lids thick with turquoise eye-shadow. Her red hair flashed in the sun. She wore a badge that told him her name was Marilyn and that she was a Carer.

"I've come for a grandma," said Rudolf.

"Lucky grandma," drawled Marilyn. She shimmied sideways to let him pass, her knuckles grazing his left buttock.

The home's interior smelled of boiled cabbage, mildew and wee. A fat receptionist with scraped-back black hair and a white overall sat behind a huge desk in the foyer tapping the keys of a computer.

"I'd like a grandma," said Rudolf.

"Any particular kind?"

"I'll know when I see her."

"It's lunchtime," said the receptionist. "Besides, we like to make them look presentable. Can you come back later?"

"I'd rather pick one now, if it's all the same. I've come a long way."

"Oh, very well then. You'll have to use your imagination. Some of them get quite messy when they're eating but most of them are house-trained. Dining room's through there." She pointed to a scuffed door at the end of a scuffed corridor. "You'll have to be firm or you'll end up with the lot of them."

THE DINING room was full of dejected grandmas playing with sausage and sloppy mash. When he walked in, they bucked up and looked at him eagerly.

Rudolf knew exactly what he wanted: a small, neat and cheerful grandma, one that wouldn't take up too much room. He couldn't bear the thought of a big fat lump of a grandma sprawled out on his cream leather furniture eating him out of house and home. On the other hand he didn't want a runt, someone who would need round-the-clock care. He didn't want a bald grandma but he didn't fancy one that was too hairy, especially in the moustache and beard department. He looked at the sea of geriatric flesh and his heart sank. The grandmas in the dining room were all of those things.

Yet over in the corner was a small, not-too-hairy grandma. He guessed she was a size 12. She wasn't exactly neat – her white hair looked electrified and she had a gravy stain down her jumper. Nor did she look cheerful but that was hardly surprising, given her circumstances. He admired her mischievous spirit; she was posting mashed potato into her neighbour's cardigan pocket. He knelt beside her chair.

"I've come to take you home with me," he said. "I'm going to look after you."

Suddenly, the room was filled with a babble of querulous voices.

"Take *me*," quavered her neighbour, "I can knit you socks and Christmas jumpers."

"No, don't listen to her. I can cook the best Yorkshire puddings and cakes."

"Please take me. I used to work in a laundry. I'll wash and iron your shirts."

"I used to be an actress. I could entertain you and make you laugh."

Rudolf shut his ears to their pleas. Gently, he prised a set of gnarled fingers from his sleeve, another from his trouser leg. He shoved his chosen grandma to the door, closed it firmly behind him and shunted her down the shabby corridor. She was very slow. Rudolf made encouraging sounds. "Come on, there's a good girl, you can do it. Not far now."

The fat receptionist was waiting for him, a sardonic smile on her lips. "Good choice," she said with a smirk, "She should scrub up nicely. She's been micro-chipped but you'll have to sign for her. Admin fees are £5 and we don't do refunds."

He scratched his name in a ledger, paid with his debit card and took his new grandma, along with a certificate of authenticity, into the sunshine where the Carer called Marilyn was smoking a fresh cigarette. He deposited his grandma on the passenger seat of his BMW with a sudden surge of protectiveness.

"Let's get you home for a nice cup of tea," he said.

For the first time she looked up at him and her blue eyes danced like sequins on a ball gown. "Have you got any gin?" she said.

And, as he drove away, Marilyn the red-haired Carer yelled after him: "Sucker!"

RUDOLF WAS happy to leave the grim old folk's home behind. As he drove away, his grandma fidgeted in her seat.

"What's the matter, my little grandma? Aren't you comfortable?"

"I need a wee," his grandma said.

"I think there's a pub somewhere along this road," said Rudolf.

The first pub they came to had a sign in the window NO GRANDMAS ALLOWED, but a mile further on was *The Dog and Whistle* which had a sign saying GRANDMAS WELCOME.

Rudolf helped his grandma out of the car.

"Isn't she sweet?" said the landlady, who had a complexion like pickled beetroot. "How long have you had her?"

"Not long," confessed Rudolf, "I'm afraid all this grandma stuff is new to me."

"Oh, they're no trouble," said the landlady, "I've got one myself. The hubby's taken her to the doctor. Her Ministry of Health certificate is due this month. Our children love her

33

to pieces. I expect your grandma will want a gin. Would you like the menu? Chef does a Grandma Special; fish fingers and spaghetti hoops with jelly and ice-cream for pudding."

AFTER LUNCH and with two double gins inside her, Rudolf's grandma fell asleep, so he parked up, left a window slightly open and popped into Marks & Spencer for size twelve clothes. With the help of an assistant called Barbara, who also was a grandma owner, he managed to spend a considerable amount of money on thermal underwear, long-sleeved nightgowns, jumpers and cardigans and skirts and trousers with elasticised waistbands.

He stowed his purchases on the back seat and let in the clutch. His grandma was snoring loudly, her head lolling against the window, a river of drool trickling down her chin. She was having a lovely dream. She was walking through a sweet-smelling wood holding a little girl's hand. The dream was so real, she could feel the girl's soft plump hand warm against her palm. The sun was shooting arrows of light through the lacy canopy of the trees and the little girl's hair shone like gold. The path of earth was warm and everywhere was the scent of wild garlic. Ahead was a dense carpet of blue and the little girl pulled her hand free and began to race towards it, her small legs as white as stripped willow.

"Grandma! Bluebells! Grandma! Grandma!"

"GRANDMA, WE'RE home, wake up grandma." Rudolf shook her gently.

Rudolf lived in a Victorian garden flat. He was very proud of its polished wood floors, original fireplaces, high ceilings and modern kitchen which had French doors leading on to a patio. There was a large spare bedroom with its own little balcony which would be ideal for his grandma. He hosed her down on the patio and left her in the sun to dry. The fat receptionist's words had proved to be right – his grandma had scrubbed up nicely. Her skin was clean and pink and her silver hair shone like a newly-minted coin.

"Where are the children?" she asked Rudolf as he settled her in a nest of cushions in front of the TV.

"There aren't any," said Rudolf, and watched in dismay as her bottom lip trembled like that of a landed trout.

"But we'll be alright on our own. I'll take you to the park and we'll eat ice-cream. We'll have a lovely time."

THEY SETTLED into a routine. When Rudolf was working, his grandma watched TV or sat in the garden, drinking gin. Once she ventured out into the street and went missing, which gave him a nasty turn. Luckily, someone had handed her into the police station, mistaking her for a stray. On Sundays they went to the park. He was amazed by the number of places that banned grandmas: cinemas, restaurants, swimming baths and stately homes – the list was endless. And, as the weeks went by, he couldn't shake off the feeling that his grandma was unhappy. She rarely smiled or laughed, not even through a party political broadcast.

ONE SUNDAY in August, Rudolf made up a picnic hamper, bundled his grandma into the BMW and drove into the countryside. He parked up and found a shady spot with willow trees and a lake where black and white ducks nested amongst the bulrushes and umber fish glided beneath the smooth green water.

He sat his grandma on a bench, tucked a rug around her knees and went back to the car for the hamper. Lugging the hamper through the trees, he heard voices. A small family had gathered round his grandma: a man and a woman and a little girl with golden hair. The girl's father was a big, blond-haired fellow who looked as if he might have sailed from the other side of the lake in a Viking ship. Her mother was small-featured and pretty, her dark hair tied back with a green ribbon. The little girl was clinging to his grandma's hand and his grandma was stroking her golden hair.

"Please, Daddy, let me keep her."

"She might belong to somebody."

"No, Daddy, she's all alone. She told me so."

"Oh, let her keep her, Tom. The responsibility will do her good. Little girls need a grandma to love."

"I'll take care of her, I promise."

"Well, it does look as if someone's dumped her."

Rudolf strode from the trees. He was about to shout: "Leave her alone! She's mine!" but something made him stop. It was as if the little girl had switched on a lamp inside his grandma's head, making her face shine with an inner glow. Quietly, he retreated and slowly made his way back to his car. And, as he drove home, the sun slid behind the horizon and bathed the sky a Renaissance pink.

God was surely in his heaven, all was right with his world, and tomorrow would be a lovely day.

Annie Shouts

Michael Yates

ANNIE was shouting full throttle. Tony couldn't make out the words at first, he was running too fast – down the stairs, one, two, three at a time, turning at the wall, scraping his elbow on the eggshell blue plaster, his ankle twisting awkwardly as he turned and hopped into the hall. *Now* he could hear the words. *Now* he could make them out. Annie was shouting: "You can't get away! Don't even think it! *Just don't!*"

He was a small, slender man and he was too busy fighting for breath. *I'm not as fit as I thought*, he thought, *I'm not as fit as I should be.*

He shouldered the door, spilled into the front room, where surely there was a weapon of some kind? The TV remote? The cocker spaniel porcelain bookends on the window sill...? He slammed the door.

Now *she* was all the way down the stairs. He could hear her breathing. She was a tall, broad-shouldered woman with long legs and big breasts, emphasised at the moment by her low-cut pyjamas. Handsome. That's how he thought about her. Not beautiful exactly. And not as young as she used to be. But good bone structure. An intelligent, sensitive face. Not sensitive *now,* of course. But handsome. Still handsome.

He ducked under the table and held his breath. She pushed open the door. She came into the room. He could see her legs. And her hands. And the thing she was holding in her hand.

She stood for a moment. She shouted: "Upstairs, downstairs! In my lady's chamber!" She shouted: "Come out, come out wherever you are! Come on out and take your medicine!"

She walked round the table. Slowly. She started shouting again. "Come on out, you coward! Come on out and take your medicine! Like a *man*! Like the man you never were!"

He said: "Look! Wait! Put it down! You can hurt somebody!"

She banged the table top. BANG-BANG-BANG!

His voice rose a little. "Don't... don't!"

She went on banging the table top with the thing in her hand. Once, twice, once again, again, again, again... ! She said: "*Oh*, we've found our level now, haven't we? Down on the floor, under the table, cringing like a dog! Well, you can't stay there for ever! I won't let you. If it's a life sentence for you, it's a life sentence for me as well, and I'm not doing with *that*!" She banged the table-top again.

He said: "Look, I'll come out if only..."

She shouted: "What would that mother of yours think of her precious son now?" She began to mimic the tones of her mother-in-law. "And here's his school report. He was always good at games. Always good at PE! Here's a picture of him in his shorts. Here's one in his swimming trunks. Look, he's still wet. And that one is when he grew his hair long. But it was only a phase, wasn't it? And here's one of him with Heather, his cousin. Sometimes I think they were more like brother and sister, they were so close. She's an air hostess now. And here's one of him with that Janet Winslow, who was head girl when he was head boy. And here's one of him at university – no, I can't remember *her* name. They seem to be enjoying themselves, don't they? I always think it's nice for young people to go out and enjoy themselves." She went back to her own voice. She shouted: "So come out and enjoy yourself, why don't you?"

He said: "I'll come out if you'll give me a chance!"

But she was doing her mother-in-law again. "I never thought he'd get married so young. Oh, I'm *sure* you'll make

38

him happy, dear. But he *is* very young." Then her own voice: "You're not so young now! Not so fit! Getting old, middle age spread, losing your hair!" And then she was imitating a man's voice. *Not very well*, he thought. "I'll be a bit late tonight, dear. Late at the office. Bit late tomorrow as well. Out for a bit on Saturday, back for tea. *Out for a bit!*" Her own voice now: "Fitness classes, down the gym, down the bloody gym. Up the bloody Alison, more like. Up the bloody Linda! And Mary! And Miriam and Gillian! And you thought I didn't know! The phone calls! The letters! You thought I wouldn't guess. Thought I was stupid! Well, I'm *not* stupid!" She ran round the table, emphasising each syllable with a crash on the table top. "I'M-NOT-STU-PID-I'M-NOT-STU-PID!"

He said: "Can't we just talk? Please!"

"This *is* talk. This is *me* talking for once!"

"Alright. Maybe it's *my* fault. *Some* of it. I mean, we can't go on like this. Let me out. Think of the neighbours. Look. I'll listen. I promise."

She said: "We're not playing a game you know. It's not bloody Monopoly. There's not a get-out-of-jail-free card!"

He said: "Let's talk. Let's say we'll talk for 20 minutes." He glanced at his watch. She stayed quiet. He said: "I feel like *The Birdman of Alcatraz*. And my legs are all stiff." She didn't answer. He began to stir. He rubbed his leg. "God, that's a bit better!"

He crawled out. He stood up. He felt sheepish. He pointed at the thing in her hand. He said: "What's that? What's that chopper doing?"

She snorted. "What's it *doing*? What *do* choppers do? Don't worry, it's just resting. Just sitting here in my hand. And it's *not* a chopper. It's a meat cleaver."

He said: "I thought we were vegetarians." He tried to laugh. He said: "Honestly, I don't know why you behave like this. I've never been violent, have I?"

"Only because I've never given you the chance!" She paused to catch her breath. "Okay. Now you're out, you better sit over there. Go on. Pull up a chair."

He did as he was told. He sat in the wooden chair with the upholstered seat embroidered with foxhunters. She sat in its twin on the other side of the carpet. He said: "Ok. Right. Where do we start?"

"Your mother. That's a good place to start. After all, it's where *you* started. She's a bitch, that woman."

He put his hands in his pockets. *Nonchalance.* He said: "Yes. I agree. Well, I don't actually *like* the word *bitch*. I think it's demeaning to women. Let's say she's a *strong* woman. But then so are you. At least that's one thing you can thank her for. She made me grow up with a taste for strong women." He paused. "Right. You've done my mum. Summed her up. Pretty well, I thought. And that cousin of mine…"

"Heather."

"And that Janet…"

"Winslow."

"Right. Neither of them meant anything. It's just that my mother expected…"

"…that you'd go out with girls. Of course. Girls who were *safe*. Non-threatening. Not like me. *I'm* threatening, aren't I? And all those girls at university…"

"They meant nothing!" He warmed to his theme. "God, they had no intelligence. No independence of thought. Not like *you*. Oh no. I don't know why women like that ever want to go to university…"

"Some women only go to get a man. They go round calling you *sister* all the time and offering you the use of their speculum for self-knowledge sessions. But they never fooled *me*. Just there to get a man. Get him into bed. Then it's…" She burst into song. "*Hi-ho-hi-ho, a housewife's life for me.*"

40

He smiled. He sang: "*Hi-diddle-de-dee.*" He'd always had a tuneful voice, though his lower registers were a bit suspect.

She said: "*What?*"

He said: "It's *hi-diddle-de-dee, a housewife's life for me.*" He said: "*Pinocchio.* Walt Disney. 1940. Only there it's an *actor's* life, of course."

"Of course." She gave her voice a sarcastic edge. "Well, *you'd* know a lot about acting!"

He began: "Well…"

She said: "Acting! Lying! Scheming! Betraying!" Her voice rose again. He realised his mistake. He should not have mentioned *Pinocchio.*

"No. You've got it wrong. It's ridiculous. I mean, all those women…"

"Linda, Mary, Gillian …" She put the meat cleaver in her lap. She ticked off the names on her fingertips. Then she picked up the cleaver again.

"No. I hardly know those women. They're workmates, colleagues, we have a drink together now and again. That's all."

"Oh, I'd like to think that. But you'll have to do better. You'll have to *convince* me." She smiled.

He took his hands out of his pockets. "Alright. That Gillian for instance. Well, it's an office, for God's sake. There are little flirtations. I mean, that's how men and women work together, isn't it?"

"I wouldn't know. I gave up work, remember? You wanted a baby. You turned the spare room into a nursery. I can see you now – painting little Paddington Bears on the ceiling. But we don't *always* get what we want, do we?"

He considered. "Yes. I was wrong to make you give up work. Now I can see how wrong I was. Now I can see what a bully I was. Self-awareness is only bought with pain, you know. Please forgive me."

"Well," she said, "I believe in forgiveness. When you're a woman, you have to." She paused. "Is that the reason you started all those affairs, then? Because we couldn't have a baby?"

He laughed. He laughed again. "Honest, there are no affairs. Really. Office flirtations, that's all. It's all banter. It doesn't mean anything. You bump into each other at the coffee machine."

Now *she* was the one who laughed. "*Bump into each other*? I'd think more of you if you admitted it. I could understand if you'd just got drunk and been tempted at the Christmas party. Just once. That would be human, that would. It's just the dishonest, calculating way you do things. That's what gets me. Yes, if there was one little lapse and if you were man enough to admit it, then I *might* forgive you. If I thought you'd told me the truth. The *whole* truth."

He faltered a moment. "Ok. Alright. Gillian."

"The tall dark one?"

"Christmas. Two years ago."

She repeated knowingly: "Cherry brandies."

He said: "No. She was drinking advocaat, I was on Stellas. And then it sort of happened."

"Sort of happened how many times?"

"Only the once. I swear. Afterwards I was so ashamed."

"She's very attractive."

"She's OK. Not as attractive as you. Nowhere near."

She said: "You're very nice to me tonight. So full of compliments." He blinked and waited for the outburst. "So!" she shouted, "You have it off with some tart that you don't even find attractive! And that little fact is supposed to make me feel good, is it?" She jumped to her feet and swung the cleaver in an arc.

He raised both hands, pushed himself back in the chair and screamed.

When he stopped, she said: "Maybe I should just cleave open your skull like a pork chop. Say something. Go on. Say something. Anything. Anything to convince me I shouldn't do that. Say something *clever*."

He said: "Alright, alright. Where do you want me to start this time?"

"Start with Alison. It's got an A. Let's do this thing alphabetically!"

"Right." With an effort, he regained control of himself. "What's this idea you've got about Alison?"

"Alison. Your precious secretary. You've been screwing that woman for the past six months. You better not lie to me now!" She waved the cleaver for effect.

He made up his mind to it. He said: "Yes. It's true!"

She burst into tears and fell back into the chair. But she still had the cleaver in her hand. "How could you? How could you do such a thing? Haven't I been a good wife to you?"

"Oh yes," he said, "yes, you have. You've been great. It was never intended as any kind of slur on you."

"*Never intended as a slur on me?* You're sleeping with your secretary and you say it's no slur on me? After all I've done! Don't I look after the house? Don't I vacuum every day? Don't I pick up all your dirty underpants? Don't I wash them for you?"

"Yes. You do. You're very clean. I like that. I admire it in you. I like having a very clean house. *And* clean underpants."

"Don't I cook for you? Don't I make all your favourite dishes? *Garlic bread!* God, it makes you stink! And haven't I been looking after your health all this time? Getting you off the cholesterol? Yogurt in the sponge cakes instead of cream? Margarine on your wholemeal?"

"Yes. Yes. I eat well. Like a king. Like a very *healthy* king."

43

She hesitated. "Is it bed then? Haven't I always tried…?"

"Always."

"But some of those things… well, *no* woman would do things like *that*! Not like in those pictures you brought home. I don't know where you get pictures like that. I don't know what woman would do such things. *I* don't. I *won't!*"

"No. I can see that."

"That Alison! She does, doesn't she? She does it all! She doesn't care what she does! I should've known. I suppose she doesn't mind that thing with the alsatian?"

"No. We've never done the thing with the alsatian. Alison is very strong on animal rights."

"It's nice to know she's got *some* principles." Her anger subsided a little. "Oh why? Why did you do it? Is she more beautiful than I am then? Is that it?"

"Absolutely not. You're far more beautiful than Alison. Any day. You're a star." He searched feverishly for an example. "You're my Julia Roberts, you are. You're my Keira Knightley. Really."

"Why then? Why did you do it?"

He spread his hands in bewilderment. "I don't know. She means nothing to me."

"Oh, I see. Because she means nothing to you, it's not supposed to bother me. That is so *insulting*! First you tell me you have it off with some tart at the Christmas party that you don't even fancy! Now you say you took up with a woman who means nothing to you. If *she* means nothing to you, what do *I* mean? Hey? Answer me that. Because if she means nothing, I must mean *less* than nothing! Is that it?"

"No, no. That's wrong. You mean *everything* to me." He searched for an answer. "*Stress*. That's it. Work. *Over*work. She worked on me." He was into his stride now. "Yes. Oh, she's a nasty piece of work. Now I think about it. She got to me. At a vulnerable time. The chief wanted all

44

those end-of-year reports and I needed to work late. Tables of figures, reams of paper..." His voice faltered. "I just thought... Oh, I don't know *what* I thought."

"You thought you could *get away* with it!"

"I thought you'd never find out. I never meant to hurt you. Honest."

She touched the tip of her nose with the fingers of her free hand. "You expect me to forgive you now? You expect me to agree a new start? Because it was just *one of those things*? Because it didn't mean *anything*?"

He looked round the room for inspiration: the Welsh dresser, the lamp made from a Chianti bottle, the bamboo magazine rack with its copies of *The Economist, The Internationalist* and *Men's Health*. He stole a glance at the cleaver. He slumped in his chair. He said: "I don't know what to say."

"Well, *I* know what to say!" She was waving the cleaver again, and he couldn't take his eyes off it. "*I* know what to say! *Wicked*, that's what I say! That's a good start, don't you think? And *selfish*. And what else would I call it? Let's see. *Deceitful*, that's another good word."

"Yes," he agreed, "yes, yes! *Selfish. Wicked. Deceitful*. Every one of those! Yes!" For a moment he thought he saw a chance. "Now, why don't you put the cleaver down?"

She looked at it as though she'd forgotten she was holding it. She laid it in her lap again. She said: "But those are *my* words. All you're doing is repeating what *I* say!"

"Because I'm agreeing with you! Don't you see? The scales have fallen from my eyes at last!" When he listened to his own voice, he hoped it sounded *truthful*. "Why don't you put the cleaver away now? Far away."

"And," she said, "you've not even apologised! You've not even said you're *sorry*!"

45

He thought hard. "Yes, I did. *Didn't* I? I'm sure I did. Anyway, I'm saying it now. Sorry! Sorry! *Sorry!*"

She picked up the cleaver. "You don't even know the *meaning* of the word sorry."

"Yes, I do. I mean, I can't quote you exactly what's in the dictionary, not with all the derivations. But of course I know what it means. *Apologies. Distress. Regret.* Stuff like that. That's what *sorry* means."

"You could at least say it as if you meant it."

He pushed himself out of the chair, fell on his knees on the carpet. He took a deep breath. He said very slowly, very deliberately: "I'm sorry. Honestly. I don't know how I can express how sorry I am. But I *am* sorry. I mean, words are meaningless to convey the *sorrow*, the *regret*, the..."

"*Distress*," she said.

"*Distress*," he said, "Words like that. Words I can't remember right now. Not all of them. But they're all here in my heart."

She stood up. She circled him. She said: "*In your heart.* I like that. I only wish I could believe it. But I can't *see* into your heart. What's hidden in our hearts is a secret, unfathomable." She placed the cleaver gently on the back of his neck. She said: "Open your shirt."

"What?"

"I said: *Open your shirt.* Just a little bit. Go on.

"What are you going to do?"

"Well, I'm not going to stare at your nipples. So I hope you're not going *all shy* on me."

He pulled aside his brown leather jacket and unfastened the top two buttons of his check shirt. She moved in front of him. She moved the cleaver from her right hand to her left. She put her right hand underneath the pale cotton of his shirt. She said: "Is my hand cold? I can feel your heart beat. It's beating very fast." She sang: "*Heartbeat, why do you flip when my baby touches me?*" She stopped singing. She

46

said: "If it's beating fast, does that mean you've been lying? Like a lie detector test?"

"No. No. Not at all."

"What does it mean then?"

"It means I'm scared."

"Well. Scared. That's what you *should* be. Scared."

"And I really am."

"Go on then. Make me believe you're sorry. Using your skill and judgement. Using your own words. Come on. I'm waiting. Convince me. You always *did* have charm. You always *were* persuasive. How do you think you got me in the first place? *He's a charmer*, I thought. *He could charm the birds off the trees*. And you could, couldn't you? *And you're still doing it!*" She shouted: "You're still doing it, you liar! Come on! Tell me you're sorry. *Make me believe it!*"

"I've never felt so sorry in all my life. I've never felt so..."

"Anguished?"

"Yes. Anguished."

"Sounds like hell."

"That's what it is. It's hell."

"It's where you belong."

"Yes. It's where I belong."

"It's what you deserve."

"Yes. It's what I deserve."

"But maybe... maybe I'll forgive you."

"Please!"

"I'm going to put this cleaver back in the bag." She pointed to an *Asda Bag for Life* on the far edge of the carpet.

"Thanks."

She crossed over to the bag and put the cleaver inside. Then she picked the bag up. She said: "I'm keeping the bag within reach. Still, you must feel a lot happier now. Now you know I'm not going to chop your head off. Or any other parts. At least, *not right away*. You can see my mood is lightening."

47

"Oh yes. I *am* happier."

"But don't get *too* happy."

"No, no, I'm trying not to."

"Because it's here at hand. It can still come out of the bag. I'll be *holding* the bag."

"Yes."

"You can do up your shirt now."

"Thanks." He did so. His hands trembled.

"I won't be rummaging in there again. Not just now. Because *now* I want to hear about the others. In detail. Names, places, how good they all were. Why you didn't think *I* was better. Let's start with Linda."

He got up off his knees. He said: "Linda?"

"Don't tell me we've forgotten Linda. The one with the hair extensions. Was she another one who didn't mean anything to you?"

"Oh no. I mean *yes*. She never meant a thing."

"Nor Mary, nor Miriam? Nor Gillian? Nor Caroline? Nor...?"

He steadied himself. He stretched. He looked at his watch. He smiled. He said: "*Hannah and Her Sisters?*" He laughed. He said: "Look. Hang on. Let's get a few things straight..."

She said: "I've *got* things straight. I've got *everything* straight."

He said: "Anyway, your time is up. We've actually run over by seven minutes. But that's OK. I won't be charging you extra."

She smiled, embarrassed. "Yes. Alright. You've been very fair. Thanks."

He said: "You know, we've let ourselves be blown way off course here. I don't think I ever had any of those women. In fact, I'm sure I never did. Not even Gillian. I know I *said* I did. But we're over-reaching ourselves. Look at it this way: where's my motivation? Hey? Answer me that. Where's

48

my opportunity? No, I'd never have the time. Not with *my* work schedule. And I'd be too tired. Don't forget: I've *studied* your husband. And the way I read his character..."

A flash of the old anger showed in her face. "The way *you* read his character? *I'm* the one who knows his character. *I* know him! Not you! You don't know him!"

"I know him from what you've told me. The secretary, Alison... yes. I can see that. That's very plausible. Bosses and secretaries. Work together. Think like a team. It happens. But not all those others. Believe me. It's a professional opinion. I'm an actor, after all. I know about character." He pointed to the bag. "The cleaver, by the way, was brilliant. It beats the stiletto shoe any day. It had me really scared. Now and again. Nice one."

She said: "You'll want your money now. It's still fifty, is it? I got it ready..." She went across to the bamboo magazine rack and produced a manila envelope. "Count it if you like."

"That's OK. We know each other well enough by now." He put the envelope in his inside jacket pocket. "Same time next week then? Is that OK?"

"Yes. Fine. You better go now. My husband's due back in half an hour. And we don't want him to know about our little arrangement, do we?" She allowed herself a smile. "It's getting so he always works late on Wednesdays. Well, you *know* that. Like every other day of the week."

She saw him off at the back door and watched him go through the gate and into the playing fields beyond. She thought: *Alison?* She thought: *Plausible?* Did he really think so? She bit her lip.

"Thanks again," she shouted after him and added: "Break a leg!"

49

Age Difference

Colin Hollis

GEORGE FOUND A PLACE just inside the entrance to the large car park, so that they could walk across and be seen.

His wife Lauren was 12 years younger than his 72, and she was good to have at his side. Slender waist, a fit and lively step, and a cloud of loose and bouncy curls that would attract attention on a 25-year-old, even if she did add colour to it these days. And confident enough to wear casual clothes and running shoes to a ladies' class reunion. On top of all his other feelings for her, she impressed him; and he felt that he matched her standard.

The restaurant was by the entrance to the complex and he could see the others, standing around the doorway, overdressed and glittering in the bright lights. The ladies had been brought by their husbands and partners, and he'd intended walking up there, letting himself get noticed, show them what a good handshake was, and he changed his mind a few strides short, and squeezed Lauren's hand and turned away.

Lauren didn't drink, and would take the Jeep home when she felt like leaving. "Shouldn't be late," she'd said, "I'll be back long before you."

He'd expressed amused puzzlement when she'd told him she would go. "It'll be entertaining," she'd said, "Men go to reunions to talk about themselves and their achievements: women go to share gossip. Should be interesting to find out what happened to everyone."

The men would mostly be a decade or so younger and might believe they looked good now in their quality suits, or at their own special events with their guts held in by a cummerbund. But a glance told him he'd wipe the floor with them at a session in the gym; the cross-trainer or bench presses or rowing machine, he'd let them choose.

He had just leaned himself on the bonnet of the Jeep when Lloyd turned up in the transit van.

Lloyd saw him, pulled up a few spaces away, got out, used his sleeve to remove a mark from the wing mirror and spoke to him across the gap. "You sure you want to do this, George? I'm ready and happy to go. I could leave you at the office. It'll be pleasant in there, busy, stuff coming in and leaving all night, folk to talk to."

It had been busy a lot lately and Lloyd was a driver short tonight, a trip into Derbyshire, and he'd told Lloyd he would go, nothing else to do for an evening, a nice change to his routines.

Lloyd was an excellent manager, partly because he fussed a lot. "You know it's over four years since you took a load out? I looked it up."

Lloyd would do that. Truth was he left most things to Lloyd these days, and he'd only been lightly involved this year, and not in the office for weeks. He'd be more comfortable on the road. "I'll enjoy myself," he told him. "New Mills, near Stockport. I've checked it out. Been before. Couple of hours each way."

"You'll have to do the unloading. There'll only be a night man on duty."

George grinned. "Don't fuss, Lloyd. It's packs of paper. I can empty the van in 20 minutes."

"You'll go up round the motorways?"

"No. A628, Woodhead Pass. I'm not doing three sides of a rectangle when I can do one. Drop down through Glossop. Same way back. I'll be home by midnight. You can send somebody round for the van in the morning."

Lloyd wasn't going to give up fussing. "There's snow forecast on the tops."

"Snow? Tonight? It's a warm night." George waved his hand vaguely at the mild air, brushed the sleeve of his pullover with the back of his fingers.

"Okay. You're the boss. You got your phone? Call in when you set off back, will you? Standard procedure. You're only a driver for the next few hours." He showed a smile, but it was a tight one.

GEORGE HAD a flask of coffee and a couple of energy bars and a map book in a canvas bag, and he got it from the Jeep. He'd drop Lloyd off back at the yard. Lloyd knew better than to offer to drive there, and walked round to the passenger side.

The cabin was clean and tidy, nothing visible but for a plastic wallet on the seat, the documents for the job. Lloyd placed the folder on his knees and leaned forward to tap the satellite navigation screen. This was one of their own vans, and Lloyd had had the systems fitted to all their own vehicles. "It's a good one," he'd said. "Worth using." *Suggesting* to his boss, rather than telling. "Got a tracker on it, so I'll know when you're there. When you're home."

"Don't need that pestering me all night. I know where I'm going." He reached to press some buttons until the map went away.

Lloyd shut up. There were lights on at the yard and the gates were open and two trucks there, drivers and mates standing and chatting. He kept the engine running, and Lloyd got out and closed the door and gave the van side two hard pats with the flat of his hand.

George made the turn and pulled out onto the road, raising a hand in an unseen salute.

ONLY JUST after seven. It was busy through town, and frustrating, until he got to the bypass and he could shuffle himself comfortable and move along. He'd not driven out this way for a while, and a pair of roundabouts on a new road layout fooled him, and he did an extra loop until he got himself going in the right direction. He passed through a couple of Pennine villages: dark stone, heavy and solid, the buildings and the folk, the roads still full, rush hour these days stretching further and further into the evening.

He was beginning one of the long climbs when the ache in his lower back became significant, and within seconds the ache had become small sharp pains down his right leg to below the knee. He'd been having this for a month or two now, a little too much time on the cross-trainer probably, trying to make up for lost sessions. Lauren had seen him wince and said it could be sciatica and he should see the doctor, get it looked at.

Sciatica was an old man's problem. This was tight glutes, a bit of tendonitis, and he'd fix it himself, work it off, or a session or two with the sports physiotherapist. It made driving in a van seat uncomfortable though.

A long queue had built up behind him, and the next rise had an overtaking lane, and a dozen vehicles powered past him, and he picked his speed up when the overtaking lane ran out.

It was glorious on the top, the hills black and outlined by a dark silver sky, a boat-shaped moon low in front and to the left, following the sun down, the curves of the red and white lights of the vehicles enhancing the scene.

And on the way down, it began to snow, small flakes, nothing the wipers couldn't cope with, but it almost annoyed him that Lloyd had been right.

Some of the bends on the west side, going down, were a bit more severe, the traffic bunched up, and he eased off and became part of a miles-long convoy. It felt good, moving along, part of the working world, getting a job done. Coming back, he'd have the road more to himself, a different feeling going home, and he'd enjoy that too.

A bit more work for the right foot and leaning

forward to peer through the snow flakes had intensified the pains in his leg, and he found himself shuffling more, trying for a position less uncomfortable. The snow was beginning to settle on the roadside.

There was a cut across into Derbyshire that he knew, but he missed it and reached the busy junctions above Manchester, the city lights a diffuse glow beyond the snow.

He knew where he was and found the road south, and was soon back in the dark between hills and woodland, the road here needing more concentration, the bends tighter. He hunched further forward, straining to see, and a pain behind his eyes added to those in his leg. He'd find some ibuprofen before he set off back.

He thought he knew the centre of Glossop, but somehow went wrong, and found himself climbing a narrow road, nowhere he believed he'd been before. He looked for a place to turn around, couldn't find one and had gone a couple of miles when he came to a cross-roads. Left seemed the obvious choice, still wanting to head south, but the twists and turns and long bends soon destroyed any sense of direction. The road surface in front of him was white now, the snow falling steadily. He realised he'd seen no other traffic for a while.

"Sat-nav," he said aloud, and stopped, a little more abruptly than he'd intended. He pressed the button and tapped the screen and there it was, a map, with a black background and yellow and grey roads and a tiny picture of his white van. How did it know to show a white van? It would have options, he thought, and Lloyd being Lloyd would have chosen the correct image.

The voice on this one annoyed him: a cultured male voice which told him to continue on the road. He did so, and he was instructed to take a right which he didn't trust but took anyway, and then a left, which he *did* trust. The next was a left at a fork and he pulled up. In the headlights, on the grass triangle between the two roads, was a scattering of broken wooden boards, the remains of a diversion sign, or road closed possibly, wide wooden strips with yellow and white diagonal markings and parts of words. Had they been discarded? Or pushed out of the way? There was no other traffic, no-one to follow. Trust the device, he thought, and went left.

He was soon climbing with only darkness in front, and continued to do so, and it quickly felt wrong so that when the slope did level out, he stopped and used the mirrors and believed that the sky was lighter behind him, the glow from a town or from Manchester, somewhere on a map. He decided to turn around at the next opportunity.

The navigation device had nothing to say.

It was another mile before he found an entrance to a field, gateposts but no gate, wide enough to back into. He went past and lined up the reverse and got it wrong and his nearside wheels dropped into a ditch and the van tilted 25 degrees. And no matter how much power or gear changing he attempted, it wasn't moving.

With the sideways tilt of the van, the door was heavy, and when his grip faltered, it fell back on to his knee with an unpleasant crack. On the ground the knee held his weight, and he went to the front of the van, some idea of filling the ditch around the wheels with stone dismantled from a wall. The engine was still running and the headlights showed the wall and the ditch and they showed the impossibility of fixing this himself. He reached down for his phone, and realised it was still in his jacket, still in the Jeep, back on the other side of the Pennines. The snow had stopped and the temperature was dropping rapidly.

He would have to walk. Back the way he'd come had shown nothing for a couple of miles, so he set off up the hill. The headlights were soon absorbed by the night, but he was still in their beam when he knew he was going to turn back, the cold, the pain, the severity of the limp overwhelming him.

The lights were dimming and the engine stuttering, and before he could get the door open, it quit, and he was in the dark, in the quiet, and in trouble. He got himself into the cab and tried the ignition, and it stayed dead, the exhaust backed into the snow and dirt at the edge of the ditch, he guessed, or the unnatural sideways tilt. If he could push the van forward, he might get the engine running, and the electrics on and some heat going, but putting his shoulder to the van would be wasted effort. He stayed where he was.

He was cold, now, very cold, and wondered about breaking open the packs of paper and surrounding himself with it, and knew it wouldn't work, and sat for a few minutes. For some reason, the pains in his leg and knee had receded, and he decided he'd really no choice but to walk and he tried to get himself up and slumped back. He'd begun to shiver quite violently.

"Get up," he said. "Keep moving. Don't sit and fall asleep." But the words weren't enough and he sank deeper into the seat, and his chin fell to his chest, and he began to cry, soft tearless sobs. After a while, he looked up and, even though the windscreen was clear, there was nothing to see. The shivering had stopped, he didn't feel too bad, he let his chin fall again and closed his eyes. His last thoughts were of disappointment at how easily he had given up.

THE VOICE, close and warm, woke him, shocked him, puzzled him. "George. Come on, wake up, help me with this," she said, a lightness there, no sense of urgency.

"Lauren? Lauren. What you doing here?" His mouth was dry, his face stiff with cold and the words badly shaped.

She didn't reply. She'd placed one foot on the sill and was trying to open the door, and she got herself partly in and turned and pushed. "Got it," she said and sat on the edge of the seat and leaned her back on him, one leg holding the door open. The air that came in with her was colder than that around him. "Told Lloyd I'd find you asleep here."

"Lloyd. Where's Lloyd?"

"Back at the office. I was just leaving the do when he phoned to say that you'd stopped in the middle of nowhere. He was worried." She was wearing his sheepskin coat over her shoulders, and she folded the collar down and looked over it at him and smiled. "He wanted to call the police and I told him: no, you'd had a problem with the van and pulled up and decided to sleep till morning. The tracker said exactly where you were and he sent me the co-ordinates, and when I put them into the Sat-nav it said I'd be here in 79 minutes. And I was. Traffic didn't seem bad. These last few roads are entertaining though."

He took a while to organise his speech. "What about the snow?" he managed.

"It's nothing. Less than half an inch. And only on this side."

"What time is it?"

"A bit after eleven. Hey, you must be cold. Let's have you in the Jeep. I phoned Lloyd when I found you, told him you were stuck in a ditch. He'll have a spare van here in the morning, get the load moved over and delivered and a rescue vehicle for this thing. I said you'd want to finish the job yourself, but I'm not giving you the choice. I'm here now and you're coming home with me."

She jumped down and pushed the door and got it fully open and turned to wait for him. The ache in his leg was a constant, and bearable, not altered by movement, but his muscles were reluctant and he took some time to get out. The drop was more than he was ready for and he jarred his ankle and winced.

"Stop whimpering," she said, and pushed the van door shut. There was light from the sky and from the snow covering, and he could see the sparkle in her eyes. "Key in the van?" she asked, and he nodded. "I'll leave it there. They'll want it in the morning."

She'd backed neatly into the space between the gateposts, the tracks in the light covering of snow showing her line. He stood, unsure of which side to take, and she gripped his elbow and led him to the passenger side. By the time he was sitting, she was ready to drive.

"Seat belt," she said. He wasn't as cold as he thought, but his hands weren't working properly, and he fumbled it a couple of times, and she twisted around and fitted it for him.

The Sat-nav came on with the ignition, and she tapped the screen until the directions for home came on. "Don't really need that," she said, pulling onto the road, "But it's best to have it on."

He didn't recognise any of the roads and didn't try. She chatted about the people she'd seen at the reunion, and mentioned a few names he believed he should know. "Didn't stay long," she told him. "They all wanted to talk about themselves, rather than share gossip. More like men, really." She aimed a quick smile at him. "Not girlie enough for me."

They were quickly through Glossop, and up above Manchester, and climbing the Pennines. The snow had collected in pale patches, the sky was clear and the stars bright.

"It's nice out here," she said, "I still think we should move out into the country. Not here, not too far, but somewhere with hills and footpaths and big skies and more room. We can go for a walk every day. I'll collect dry grasses and display them in my vases. You can build yourself a nice big workshop."

She waited for an answer, didn't get one. "Well, we can think about it. No hurry. We've got plenty of life left." Without looking, she reached over and gave his arm an affectionate punch, and drove on into the night.

A Stolen Night

Shree Ganguly

K looks up stealthily. He cannot remember last when he has seen something so young, so taut. He can count the vertebrae on her back, long and serrated like a gold necklace.

She turns around, her head tilted to one side, breathing deeply, almost unaware of the room, of him, of the utter stillness apart from the slow whirring fan overhead. "Come here," she says.

She is unrestrained like her name, *Arundhuti* – boundless. But everyone calls her Dhoop, which also has a meaning – the scorching sun, scalding and metallic. "Look," she says. She points outside.

At a distance the silver sea meets the lilac sky, the long stretched-out colourless beach stares back like a blackened slate. Mandarmani – neither here nor there, somewhere nestled in a long forgotten world: just the sea and the sand and the coral crabs.

The fireflies waft around the windows, burning dots that set her hair alight – it barely touches her shoulders, her neck is too long.

She gestures with her hands, her eyes wide, as if she has just woken up from sleep. She holds him up like an equal: straight, tall, strong and although she's high from the coke, she stands on her toes and kisses his eyelids, half dangling from his arms, her feet on top of his. "Has anyone told you that you have the longest lashes and the longest legs, K?" she laughs.

"Isn't that what *I* am supposed to tell *you*?" He laughs in spite of himself.

He holds back as long as he can, passive as her body rises and falls on him like a watery curtain. They have always made love in darkness, on stolen nights, nights stolen from Tina, his wife.

His finger runs through her spine – the rigid bones, the smooth-hard flesh – and it reminds him of London somehow, of the Natural History Museum: the bare, leafless trees filled with dry brittle nests from the large glass windows and Ronnie wearing his best sad-puppy look, wanting a pet dinosaur.

"But why can't I have one, Daddy? I can count them all. Look. I know they have 300 *ver-tee-brae*. But why can't I have a model like that in our house?"

He can almost hear Ronnie's soft cooing voice: his son's sudden musings, his whims, his child's urges echoing through the semi-darkness, the bones, the feathers and the corpses.

For a moment he's certain that Ronnie's in the next room, that he's afraid, that he'll cry out, shattering the silence; and the night will end up like it invariably does, with his wife turned on one side and the Ayah cradling the shrieking boy in some room, and K smoking out his last cigarette on the veranda, the Night Jasmine smelling stronger, fiercer, sweeter, dying slowly.

For a long time he thinks of tyrannosaurus rex, it's the fiercest of them all. A carnivore. He almost stifles himself with the pillow so as not to taint the silence, it's so pure, so *empty*. That is all he feels – half molten inside and half crumbling.

He chooses not to see Dhoop's face till the very end. Till she cries out softly like a kitten, her nails digging deeper and deeper into his hair, it's only then he looks up at her face, red splodges down her cheeks, like the roses that Tina orders from Odorantes in Paris. That is when he begins to feel a connection, like a silken thread, a fleeting moment that says life might mean something after all.

He cries afterwards in the washroom, tears streaming down his face. He has never felt so strong or so weak. He has never before let himself feel so disconnected. So deflated. He feels as if something has broken inside, given away after all these years.

Next moment, he's all man. Calm, strong, collected.

As he gets out, still moist from splashing cold water, the shadow of a beard just beginning on his sharp angular face, Dhoop says, her voice hoarse: "Let's go for a drive."

He can see her sitting on the bay window, already a stranger, the thread half-snapped. "What? Now?"

"Yup!"

"Not now. We'll be seen."

"So what? Let's just go. *I'll* drive."

He thinks of her roommate, but she can read his mind quicker than he can think. There is nothing slow and languorous about her like his wife – Tina's etiquette, her sense of poise, the little mini she drove around Oxford when she studied there with him, all messy hair and pale skin, now jaded and distant.

"My roommate's as good as dead, she's super stoned... She'll not be back till morning" Dhoop laughs. And then with one eyebrow raised, her left foot dangling from the window sill ...

"I thought you *Bongs* are forward, so what's stopping you now? I want a drive and if you don't, I'll drive out myself." She tries to light a roll-up. Her hands shake a little, restless, clumsy even, but sharp as a streak of lightning.

"Are you sure you should mix this stuff?" he asks.

"What? After snorting?" She laughs at his ignorance, at his age. "It goes out pretty fast. I'm clean now, I need a drink, a quick one. Come on then." Her words overlap, keeping up with her pace.

They creep through the narrow hotel corridor, limp roll-ups in hand, whisky flask in her bag. He feels uncertain, young, aroused once again by the smells – sea, salt, froth, whisky, weed.

"I feel like cake,' she says, biting her lips. "I feel like cake. Get me something quick, I feel so hungry! Cake... *cake*!!!" She cries out on a whim like a child, sticking out her lips.

He laughs as he listens to the soft rumbling sounds of her tiny waist. "It's a little too late for cake, Dhoop. The shops are closed."

"There must be some bread in the mini-bar. Can you get me some?'

He hesitates. Is it safe to leave her outside? It's too secluded – the whole of Mandarmani, not a soul loitering around at night, just the buzz of the insects and the distant roar of the waves, pitch dark apart from the fireflies.

"You get in the car." He hands her the keys, and on second thought leads her to the gleaming black Audi himself. "Stay here, lock the car, I'll be back in a second." He walks back, his body aching. He has been driving four hours, after work, all the way from Kolkata in the mad traffic. And now he feels isolated as if he has been transported to another world. Invisible, invincible. Nobody knows he's here, and yet they'll know in the morning when they see his car, *if* they see his car at all; he has thought of an excuse as to why he has come, a story, just in case.

When he returns with a piece of toast and honey, she's on the driver's seat ready to roar.

He cannot allow her to drive. He knows she's far too drunk, uncontrollable, her sense of restraint has crumbled like his own crumbling insides, she has lost her fear of him, she's 20 years younger, fresh as the night jasmine and just as potent. In the morning when things get real, he'll be the boss again.

Now she drives callously, laughing all the way on the straight, endless stretch of empty beach, 13 kilometres from the beginning till the end. She brakes suddenly, in the middle of nowhere, the soft sand spattering round the wheels...

"What now?"

"I need to pee."

"What? No, not here. It's not safe to stop."

"I need to. I'm hurting."

"Okay, quick."

He shifts to the driver's seat quickly while she's gone, his head reeling. He reaches out for the bottle of water as she squats down at a distance in the middle of the empty beach, the waves lapping up her feet, the moon one-fourth eaten up, the sand moist. He wants to remain in the moment but his mind wanders.

He thinks of Tina, just as undignified as Dhoop looks now, her tiny white feet over her head, her little face pale and anxious, her sweaty hands on his and the doctors sowing the seed. "A dot, that's what it is, the beginning of life and it's inside you now. Be optimistic Mrs Sen. It'll work out this time, it'll find its way. Remember: lots of chocolates and happy thoughts."

Later, when they sit around at a cafe near Park Street, Enya playing in the background, "Only Time", Tina whispers like in the song. "Maybe third time lucky." She laughs bitterly, not believing the words herself.

Dhoop has forgotten to put on her tiny denim shorts; they lie on the beach like a woman's upturned backside, metallic blue like the water and shining. He gets them back, holds them up, time slipping through the holes like sand. For a moment he forgets what he has been doing Monday, Tuesday, Wednesday; he remembers the right now, Friday night. A stolen night.

She kisses him softly all over again, and the car shakes a little as they make love, the little black box littered with her things: purse, bag, lip-gloss, sandals.

This time he shouts louder than her and begins to laugh, his happiness ringing through the silence. But, as they rest for a few minutes, he feels ashamed, reduced to nothing, the thread snapped twice. The silver sea spilled out on the midnight sky.

She gulps some whisky neat from the flask, fire down her throat. "Let's go. What are we waiting for? Let's get to Mohona. You have to see it before you leave, it's where the river meets the sea."

He drives hard as if the wet sand cannot hold him back, nothing can. She likes his hands, his nails dull white against his wheatish skin. She likes his smells, old leather against wood, a hint of lemon and fraying books. She likes his cigarettes, the faint smell of ash that he leaves behind, but most of all she likes the sharp bony cleft on his chin. She strokes it now and then, the hard line dividing his face, clashing against soft eyes. The spiritual and the cerebral and the carnal, all muddled up. She enjoys this rift, his books, his strength, his weakness.

"My mother knows your wife," she says softly, looking up at him, "They swim at Tollys, but they've never spoken."

She almost tells him what she thinks of Tina: the measured dimpled smiles, the carefully coiffured hair, the subdued hint of private blends. She wonders if *he* feels the same.

"You Bengalis have such a bong-complex," she says quickly, changing the topic, biting the tip of her tongue, slightly flustered. She rubs her nose, it's still Rudolf red from the coke.

To her relief, he laughs and then pulls her closer, his left arm on her shoulders just for a fleeting second. She opens the glove compartment. "What are you reading?"

"*Narcissus and Goldmund,*" he says. It's a leather bound copy. She takes in the deep, half-musty yellowing smell; she traces the rough white pages, the little black words. No one reads Hesse at hers, no one she knows reads Hesse, except for him of course. On the front page a sprawling purple-blue writing:

' *Darling K, hope you enjoy reading this as much as I do just looking at it. Love Tina.*'

Expensive ink. Dhoop laughs at the thought of reading sheepishly under the sheets – she gets the same 'high' out of him; he is her book, her own leather-bound copy.

"You need to shave thrice a day," she says, rubbing her burning cheeks. "See what you've done to me."

Her words are slurring slightly, flitting from dreams to reality, time slipping out in chunks and slices, days and moments passing without momentum. Holding the book to her chest, she almost falls asleep, her mouth open, her head swaying from side to side, feeling that absurd half-fulfilled emptiness that comes with the end of another day.

"What's a Bong complex?" he asks just to wake her up, his eyes on the stretch of sand ahead, on the dashboard, full of tiny moving shadows, firefly shadows, luminescent like candles in the dark. Her head swims a little. She stretches out feverishly like a cat, her long limbs dwarfing the car. She feels the rough matt black dashboard with her feet and her slim golden hands reach out for the roof.

"You know all about Bong complex. You're only teasing me." She almost tells him what she thinks but asks instead: "What's the book about?"

"I don't know. I've read it twice, I think it's about emotions and intellect, the masculine and feminine forces, the

65

truth behind existence I suppose... But it's more complex than that."

She likes it when he talks like this, of literature, of music, of art. He thinks differently. After all, he is the creative head, the Director. She likes the sound of his post, the power that comes with it.

She's only an apprentice; she doesn't even get a salary – it's K who encourages her to gain experience, to find *perspective*. The darkness and the sea make her think; she enjoys the silence of her thoughts as much as he does; it's a quiet camaraderie. Her mother can never even begin to understand this. She thinks of her mother at the salon; that is where she spends most of her time, someone massaging the ample folds of her flesh.

She thinks of her mother's generosity, her enormous tips: the malevolence behind the crunchy green notes. She has seen money – the best and the worst of it.

"You know my mother wants me to marry a Bengali boy, a Rasgulla....' she laughs, teasing him, the taste of the juicy white sweet filling up her mouth, "Can you believe that? A Maru marrying a Bong?"

She thinks of the hard-core conservative Marwari business community that she belongs to, the survivors. And the Bengalis themselves, dreamers like K, chaotic. The city is rifted. In fact she is not sure if she belongs to Kolkata at all, or anywhere else for that matter. She laughs emptily, lets her thoughts waft out with the fireflies, the burning in them as inconsequential, as humdrum, as ceaseless as their dance of death.

On an impulse, she pulls up the t-shirt and bares herself, moving instantly to a different space. She sits up rigid, hardened to the core, unashamed, unfaltering. She rejoices in the effect of her flesh; she almost begins to regurgitate her past, the disjointed pieces of the city fall out like dried flowers, till she is left bereft.

"And what do *you* want?" K asks.

"Nobody's asked me that before. I don't know what I want, a Rasgulla maybe?" She laughs but he turns away; she is suddenly afraid to face him. "Do you want me, K?"

"Put on the T-shirt. We've almost reached,' he says. She obeys. "Mohona reached," he says, braking soundlessly. She opens the door but he jerks her back roughly. "Stay inside. You understand this place is deserted at night."

She hesitates for a second and then jumps out, the breeze catching her hair. It's almost three o'clock and still very dark, as if she's suddenly turned blind. It's nothing but darkness and the ceaseless whirring of the insects. She looks around disappointed, drinks greedily from the flask, emptying it, the liquid racking up her insides. He holds her steady from behind as she sways. "It's nothing but darkness."

He takes her in his arms. Sudden tears well up in her eyes, salt seeping through her nose, her mouth, her face. She feels displaced. "I wanted you to see what I saw," she says, holding back her tears, her hands clenched. She is surprised at her own reactions, one part of her holds still, checks herself.

She had come here this morning, with her roommate, to Mohona – the confluence, the origin, where the river meets the sea. The white spread-out beach on one side, the river on the other, its banks shaded with acacia trees, and further on the empty island of Tajpur. She had longed to go to the island; she had longed to feel its solitude, the white sand dotted with scarlet crabs. Her colleagues had gone to Tajpur by boat, but she had refused to go with them. She had waited alone smoking a joint, gazing at the blue sky, the river, the sea, the dim lights on the fishing boats, flickering in and out, welcoming dawn, unapologetic to have been born a woman. Unashamed.

He knows she'll be fine. He lets her drive because that'll take her mind off. She drives carefully, despite her inebriation, her movements controlled. She is gauging herself, every action, every breath – a controlled resignation. At least there is no traffic. Not a soul, nothing she can bump into, just a dark dreary strip of beach spread out like a bare arm. He scans the vista, both the road and her. At times he thinks of Ronnie's nightmares, his scared little face and his constant sense of detachment. He feels guilty for not trying enough, for not trying at all.

"I wish I could adopt too," Dhoop says suddenly, mockingly. "I'd adopt a girl, if I could. Why did you choose a boy?' She wants him to get angry, like she is. He understands, he somersaults into his past for shelter, his Oxford days. How he and Tina would venture out at night; the books left behind in their messy rooms; she'd line her stomach with *fromage frais* on crusty toast before a drinking binge: vodka, rum, wine, cocktails, anything went. Although she would never dream of being so wasted, of peeing in the middle of a deserted beach, she'd line her lips with rose petal salve and spray *Annick Goutal - Eau d'hadrien* later, to get rid of the smells.

He ponders the definition of perspective, angle, vista, attitude.

Then Dhoop begins to laugh for no reason. She looks back in form, her head swaying from side to side. Perhaps she has hurled her anger away at the rocks. She begins to recite one of her ridiculous poems that she reads out to him when she's drunk enough.

'Our jeans make love together
In the washer!
Entangled blue legs,
Floating out our wasted cells.
As we wait for this cycle to stop
As we wait for this cycle to end...'

"That's my newest poem, my ode to us", she laughs hysterically and he laughs with her, thinking of the warm hotel room, the tousled bed. He knows he'll have to sneak out again before morning. He dreads the drive back but the 'now' feels alive, beautiful, refreshed.

It's the darkest part of the night, about half past three, when the car skids a little, wavers to the wet part of the beach. She pulls to the left, she struggles to make it move again, she uses all her strength; he is ready to jump out but the car begins to move again. She laughs aloud, happy, triumphant. The beach looks even more deserted without the fireflies, stretched out far and wide, not a single light shining anywhere, not a sound. They could be driving anywhere; they could be driving through time and space. At a distance a shadow appears. A tree? What is it? As they approach closer it seems something like a man waving, a man in distress. K feels his heart racing, pounding, his hands grow cold.

"Dhoop, don't stop. It must be a drunk or something, just drive on, just don't stop here!"

Two men waving frantically come closer, unafraid of the slow moving car. One comes running right at the front and the other goes around the back. She brakes suddenly, afraid to run them over, her eyes wide, her mouth open.

One of them knocks on the glass, "Plee-ee-ase help us! We're tourists, we got robbed right now. Help us."

K looks at them in the face, one is younger than the other and darker, they look like tourists; half-open rucksack on one of their backs. But before he can answer, they have already opened the back door and jumped in. It all happens so quickly, half a minute, maybe less, even before he can press the lock button, before he can get his orientation back. The alcohol and the weed have slowed him down more than his age.

"Get out!" K growls softly, menacingly, desperately. Staying on his seat, holding on to Dhoop's fingers. They feel cold with sweat. He pushes the man behind him. In a flash, the other one takes out a knife and holds it from behind right into Dhoop's chest. She stays still, quiet, her hands protecting her face, and then cries out suddenly, something in between a scream and a shudder. She struggles.

The man hits out. K tries to reach the man behind Dhoop. He thrashes out at him, the knife falters for a second till K feels a cold metallic snout at the small of his back. They are wily, their tactics practised.

"Do as I say, turn around towards Mohona. We'll drive to Tajpur. *Now*. We'll go for a fucking long drive," the other man orders. He has taken out a gun. K cannot believe it, but its feel is unmistakable.

"The island? But that's 25 kilometres. I don't have that much fuel. Take our money and let us go." He orders, falters, stammers, begs. "Please, take everything." He takes out his wallet, opens it and Tina stares out from inside, her skin pale as moonlight.

Their faces are shaded, mangled in his mind. One is Mr Darkness, the other Mr Light, one of them hits him at the back of his head, a stinging blow, and then he feels a hand round his neck. "Another woman, you mother fucker! One woman in the wallet, the other in the car!" laughs Mr Light. He shoves K roughly, the gun still at his back. Dhoop turns the car around, obeying them.

They drive in silence for a few minutes till the younger man snaps: "Whiskey huh? Imported whisky and drugs!" He smells of cheap country liquor, his breath stale, his face almost in Dhoop's hair. He makes lewd jokes at her. "Kali kaloti" he hisses in accented Hindi - *dark and ugly*. He spits at the back of her neck, and spits again, moving forward at the side of her face. "Whore!" he says, "You deserve to be splayed. You deserve what you're going to get."

They cannot be locals, Bengalis can hardly ever speak Hindi. Who are they? Criminals? People from the slums?

Tourists? They snarl and threaten all the time; they intimidate more with gestures and smells: the smell of threat, the smell of fear.

"Get out of the car!" snarls Mr Darkness to K. "Get the fuck out!" and hits him with the barrel at the side of his head.

"Let her go, take the car... take everything!" K pleads, one last frantic attempt, reduced to nothing, his hands folded, twisted, "Please! Please!" his voice a whimper, "Please! Please! Please!"

She cries out on cue: "Please! Please! Please!" she begs, "Please! Please! Please! Plee-ee-ase!" Her pride crushed to nothing, he has never seen her like this, he has never seen himself like this.

"Step away from the car or I'll shoot," says Mr Darkness.

K contemplates; he has less than a minute to act, to do something. He steps back a little further, his arms outstretched in the shade of the acacia trees, feigning resignation. "Bend down, you rascal!" says the other man on Dhoop's side. "Shoot him! Shoot the bastard! Shoot right into his balls!"

K makes a desperate lunge at Mr Darkness, one last ditch attempt, taking him by surprise. The man holds onto his gun. He shoots out suddenly, instinctively. Two distinct shots before they speed away with Dhoop, leaving K lying face down on the beach.

K lays low for a minute, his eyes half closed, his body shaking. Shocked, violated. He feels all over, he knows he could have been hit although he feels nothing yet, just a strange numbness, a tingling on the soles of his feet. In the clarity of the moment he can hear the waves, the chirping of the birds roused by the shattered silence.

He has a torch with him, somewhere in his pocket, he has left the mobile behind, not that there would be a signal here, now. He scampers up painfully, nothing is broken, nothing splintered. Mr Darkness has missed, lucky twice. K laughs a little. He walks back like a ghost in the direction of the hotel. After a few minutes he turns around in the opposite direction and begins to follow the tyre marks on the sand, walking towards Mohona and then he begins to run.

His shoes come in the way, he gets them off, throws them away, his feet sinking into the cold wet sand. He is an expert runner, his stance strong as steel. He runs on instinct, without thought or feeling or emotion. After about a mile, he sees a black dot, the car parked at a distance, its doors splayed open.

He waits at first; and then, when nothing moves, he approaches it with caution. He looks inside, no sign of them, all three of them gone, her bag, her slippers, the flask – everything. Vanished into the night. On the back seat. where she had thrown them, he finds her denim shorts, the only sign of her. He paces about for a minute, terrified, ashamed, then picks out a golf-stick from the back of the car. Tina likes him to play golf although it bores him to death. He runs ahead a little, his mind whirring like the fiery insects, torch in one hand, stick in another. Stick and torch. He almost laughs at himself, the vision of an ancient prehistoric man carrying a stick and fire. He has nothing else to offer but his strength, his manliness.

"Dhoop!" he shouts frantically, desperately, "Dhoooooop!"

They cannot have gone far, not further than those acacia trees. But as he runs towards them, the trees move further and further and further away, their leaves whispering softly in the wind, teasing him. At a distance he sees a light, perhaps a kerosene lantern. A fisherman's hut! He runs faster but it's farther than he thinks. He bends down, a little exhausted; lies down flat on the sand: his mouth open, his eyes wet with tears. He feels the bump at the back of his head.

And then a sudden faded light bursts through the sky – the sun rising softly. The sea looks silver pink.

He thinks of the snow, the soft alpenglow lighting up Tina's face on their honeymoon in Norway, snow-clad peaks and sunrise and sex. Tiny snowflakes nestling on the open branches, tiny snowflakes swirling languidly on open palms, tiny snowflakes like silver glitter on Tina's long dark hair. The thought jolts him like her whispers echoing back and forth from the orphanage in Kolkata – "I know the donation will help you, Mother Superior, there'll be more of it later. We'll have to have a boy, you understand, an heir. Healthy, light skinned, he has to fit our profile, you have to look out for what we want and – let's be practical, this is not just about love, is it?' He remembers Tina's dimpled smile lighting up her face and Ronnie, their 'made to order' child.

He walks back towards the car; he'll have to get it started. They must have tried to speed away and now the wheels have stuck firmly into the sand. He fumbles for a moment and then throws Dhoop's metallic denim shorts as far as he can towards the sea. He can imagine the waves crashing them; filling up their holes, slipping through and through, he can imagine the fish nibbling them, the gaudy molten-metal blue. He dreads to think of the inevitable. Of Dhoop, of what has happened, of what *is* happening. He absolves himself in the car, cleaning the seats, the mats, checking the tyres. What will he tell Tina? What will he tell his team? No one even knows he's here. He's not even supposed to be here.

His mind flits back to Dhoop again. To them making love in the little candle-lit room, not that long back. Of them having a fight. Not talking. Not making up before sleep. Looking away from each other in bed and then just like that in the middle of the night, the soles of their feet rubbing against each other, suddenly, softly; and their displaced, forever conflicting worlds assuaging into one at that very moment. He has never felt a feeling more intimate and he knows he never will.

He's already making up stories in his mind, wondering how Dhoop can feature in them, if at all. He begins searching for his shoes and finds them at a distance. Tightening his shoelaces, dusting them off a little, he thinks aloud: "Eternity is but a mere moment, just long enough for a fucking joke."

He thinks of Hermann Hesse. He remembers the book. Terrified, he searches for it but it's nowhere – she must have taken it with her. His heart sinks.

But just as he looks up on the dashboard, where the shadows of the fireflies had danced not that long back and transferred to her tiny golden feet like henna patterns made of light, he finds it lying on one side, its dark leather cover acting as a camouflage.

He laughs in relief.

Still Life with Fruit

Philip Andrews

"WOULD YOU LIKE some fruit, grandad?"

The basket stood on the glass-topped table beside the french windows and, because he was looking at it *contra jour*, the reflection was more colourful than the fruit itself. In *his* house it would have been unloaded haphazardly into a bowl as it came out of the supermarket bag, but here each item had been precisely arranged. There was deliberation behind the carefully careless construction of oranges and grapes in front of him, the pale ochre blemishes dripping like paint down the blood-red apple skins. He knew she had assembled them.

"No, thank you. It would be a pity to spoil such a perfect still life."

But *she* had no reservation. She picked out an apple for herself and came and sat beside him on the sofa. He could see the chisel-marks her even teeth cut into the pure, white flesh. His own teeth were less well-preserved, which is why he kept his lips together when he smiled at her.

"Did you know that Caravaggio was the first person to paint a still life?" she asked. "That was a basket of fruit."

They had finished lunch and soon he would take her to the station for her sixth-form trip to London: the Tate, the National Gallery. His wife and daughter had gone to Leeds to sniff their wrists around the perfume counters in Harvey Nicks and sip large, cold glasses of Marlborough *Sauvignon Blanc* over lunch. His son-in-law was appearing for the prosecution in that murder trial in Sheffield that was all over the media at the moment.

"Surely somebody had painted still life before that?" he said.

75

"Before then, everyone painted religious subjects or Greek myths. Caravaggio made the leap forward and other artists followed. That's how it always is with movements in art – the pre-Raphaelites, then the impressionists, then the cubists."

In someone else her age, he would have seen a precocious brat, but she was his grand-daughter and therefore could do no wrong. She would get into Cambridge. She had a genuine passion for art and she knew her stuff.

"You've spoiled the composition now," he said. "You'll have to rearrange it."

"Nobody does still life now, grandad. Now an artist would use the apple core to make a conceptual statement."

She already knew far more than he did about the history of art. When he was her age, the only painting he could name was *The Haywain*, seen on a chocolate box at Christmas. He had left school at 16 to become an apprentice draftsman in the offices at the local colliery – drawings of roof supports and conveyor belts – but having seen the future, and that it wouldn't work, had moved into designing supermarkets, and had done very well. What little he now knew about art had come mostly from taking his grand-daughter to galleries.

But he said: "The first still life I ever saw was out on the wall in my grandparents' back yard. That had an apple core in it."

"Grandad!" she said sharply, as though she were telling off a child. It was the same mock rebuke she made when he told her every New Year's Eve that he had just met a man with as many noses as there were days in the year, or used his mock ventriloquism to pretend that her cat could talk. His playing the eccentric old man always amused her. She *knew* he was playing at it, of course, and he knew that she knew. It was their little game, something they would always have in common, that spanned the generation gap, just as he had once bonded with his own grandparents, linking hands across the years.

On this occasion, though, he was not joking but reminiscing.

"It's true," he said. "It was in a white enamel bowl with a dark blue rim. The enamel was chipped and the bowl was going rusty. There were apple cores in there and the ribs of a cauliflower from which the white part had been eaten, potato peelings, carrot tops..."

"Very *avant garde*," she laughed, still thinking he was playing the fool with her.

"Not at all," he said. "It was an early form of recycling. My grandma put all her kitchen scraps in that bowl and left it on the wall by the gate to be collected by a man who kept a pig on his allotment. He boiled it all up and turned it into pig-swill: came round every day with a wooden barrow with a squeaky wheel, so the still life was always changing. In return he sometimes left a cabbage he'd grown, or a few sticks of rhubarb. Then I was allowed to sit on the wall with some sugar in a cup and dip the rhubarb in and eat it. When he killed the pig, he hung the carcass up in his shed and split it open right down the middle, so you could see all its intestines and tubes, like a map of the London Underground."

She giggled. "What a lovely image. Francis Bacon could have painted that with great squeezes of oils straight from the tube."

"That would have been very apt," he said, but she had not made the connection between subject matter and artist's name. She was not yet quite the finished article.

Percy the cat, who could not really speak, had materialised and was rubbing round her legs, wanting to go into the garden. She got up and went to the french windows to let him out. The smell of the grass that the gardener had cut into neat, two-toned stripes entered the room. There had been no grass in his grandparents' yard: only the smell of smoke from the coal fire.

"Were you poor, grandad?" she asked reflectively as she sat beside him again.

"I never thought so, but that was probably because we always seemed happy. Perhaps *you* would think we were poor. My grandfather earned £5 a week working down the mines. He would come home with a big white £5 note and a few shillings in his pocket. His face would be black with coal dust, but the skin round his eyes was still white, like a panda. Then he got into this big tin bath in front of the fire in the kitchen and grandma poured hot water over his head to get him clean."

Her lips made a pouting grin. He knew she did not believe him, thought that he was kidding her again. But that was all true as well.

"That's something you could tell them at your Cambridge interview. They like a bit of rough, to feel they're not completely out of touch with 99 per cent of the population, even though the evidence against them is overwhelming. Just don't mention that you live in Harrogate and that your dad's a barrister."

The cat was already at the window, wanting to come in again. She picked him up and stood facing her grandfather with Percy in her arms. Her jeans were ripped above both knees. That would have been a source of shame in his youth, but for her it was a fashion statement. She had named the cat after one she had seen in a Hockney painting in which the woman holding it was standing beside her husband in front of french windows in a fashionable London house. So here was life imitating art. She looked so beautifully unspoiled, standing there stroking the purring animal, that he had to put from his mind how quickly that would change. He thought instead how strange it was that Percy was also the name of the man who kept the pig. He seemed to remember that he drove a steam locomotive that hauled the coal wagons at the pithead.

"Where did they live?" she asked.

"My grandad and grandma? In a little mining town between Wakefield and Castleford." It was only about 20 miles from where he now sat talking to his grand-daughter but it could have been on a different continent. And it *was* another century.

"There was a famous sculptor from Wakefield. Barbara Hepworth. We went to her gallery from school."

"And another from Castleford," he said. "Henry Moore's father was the manager of the coal mine where my grandfather worked."

Her expression changed to one of genuine surprise, as though he had unexpectedly done something rather clever. He knew she loved him, of course. Not in the way she loved her parents, or would love some man, or several, in the future, but he knew he was fairly high up the scale of love on which fond and undemanding grandparents are measured.

"Awesome! Did your grandad know him?"

The awe came from the same root as that look. He had suddenly moved several points up her scale of Intellectual Respect, on which he suspected he had scarcely figured before. (The small standing he commanded in his own field did not travel beyond the offices and meeting rooms of his peers.)

"I doubt they moved in the same circles, although grandad was a sculptor of sorts. He was a blacksmith. He mended the machinery they used to cut and shift coal underground. He made things for my grandmother out of bits of waste metal – tongs for putting coal on the fire, a shovel to scoop up the ashes – beautiful things, heavy, they felt comfortable in your hand. You could see the tiny weld-marks on the steel. And he made toasting-forks out of plaited wire.

Three prongs, and you stabbed the bread with them and held it over the red hot embers. Best toast I ever tasted."

She made that little *moue* again. This time it was incomprehension that there had ever been a world in which the electric toaster had not been invented.

He wanted to tell her more, about how his grandparents had eventually had a proper bath plumbed in at their two-up, two-down terraced house and given the old galvanised bath to Percy, who used it as a copper in which to boil up the swill; and how the street outside was unsurfaced and when it rained they would use the shovel he had made to take cinders from the grate and go out to fill in the potholes. But he was afraid of boring her, sounding like a sad old fart.

"Sorry," he said. "I'm sounding like a boring old fart."

"No," she said, sitting beside him again. "I like to hear about it. I want to know before…"

"Before I'm dead," he laughed.

She pouted again and put her hand lightly on his arm. She did not wish to entertain that thought, and he took that for a declaration of love. He tipped his head back against the cushion and closed his eyes. The darkness, paradoxically, lit up more of the pictures he kept hidden away inside, and he brought some of them out to show her.

"We used to slide down the pit tip on tin trays, and when we got home and took our shoes off, our feet were black with dust up to the ankles."

"What's a pit tip?"

"The spoil heap where all the overburden from the coal seam was dumped – a great mountain of slate and rock and dust. They could be a hundred feet high and a mile long. There was one practically at the bottom of our yard."

Telling her all this seemed like relating life with the Marsh Arabs – a completely different culture long gone, that now existed only in a small back room in the museum of his mind. Revisiting it was like waking from a dream – when you tried to go back, it had evaporated and all you had left were a few random images. Maybe there were some photographs in public libraries and archives, or a few amateur watercolours of winding gear or of pit ponies brought up to the surface to graze. Perhaps one day his grand-daughter would curate an exhibition of them. *That* would be something.

"I've never seen a pit tip," she said.

"They've all been 'reclaimed' now. But when your dad drives you down the A1 to Cambridge, look out for the smooth, grassy hills near Featherstone and Pontefract. They've got sheep and trees on them now, but there's no hiding what they were. And the tin sheds they call business parks have been put up where the pit yards used to be."

She lay her head against his upper arm, something she had done ever since she was a small child, when her parents and her grandparents were her entire world. He wondered when she would grow out of it. He was surprised she hadn't already, but she still had some of the unfeigned innocence of childhood about her, despite her precocity. It would get knocked out of her at Cambridge, of course; but for the moment, as they sat in silence, it seemed as though they were both part of some profound and everlasting... *what*? Some sort of changing but stable continuum, perhaps, that carried some kind of meaning that would one day be understood? A bit like the history of art? He had no idea, but this was perhaps as close to knowing as he would ever come. How could you live as long as he had without finding out what it was all about? She, of course, was still young enough to believe that one day she would.

He had always found this modern, Danish sofa uncomfortable, and strands of the girl's hair were tickling his cheek. But he dared not move for fear of disturbing the moment. He gazed down at the top of her head and thought how ironic it was that for all her love of fine art, her appearance was beautifully artless – tall and mannequin-thin, delicate features, skin that had no need of make-up. Her long hair was that Anglo-Saxon dirty-blonde, streaked naturally with sun-bleached strands that fell across her face so that she had to keep pushing it back. Neither painter nor hairdresser could ever replicate that. It reminded him of his grandmother washing her own long hair over the thick pot sink in the corner of her living kitchen. The nape of her neck was just like his grand-daughter's – another fragment of continuity in a changing world. He knew he was on the cusp of some great change, a new movement in both their lives, and he knew he would come to embrace it. But not just yet...

Then Percy jumped into her lap and broke the spell.

"You'll enjoy Cambridge," he said. "Punting on the river, picnics on the Backs like that painting with the naked girl and the men in bowler hats."

"*Le Dejeuner sur l' herbe,*" she said with what sounded like a perfect French accent.

"That's the one. But if I hear *you've* been taking your clothes off, young lady, there'll be trouble."

She laughed and hugged him. She had already decided on the subject of her dissertation: the effect of Mediterranean light on the palettes of Cezanne and Matisse, or some such thing. She would live in the sun, the Riviera, moving on again.

Yet as he sat there with her head against his arm, he knew there was a sense in which life moved on but didn't change. You just kept adding to it, like buying pictures for a gallery, and you could keep going back and looking at the ones you most enjoyed, often with deepening appreciation. For some reason the thought produced an image of tramping home with his grandfather from a football match at Huddersfield in winter, which he always associated with that painting of hunters in the snow. Bruegel, that was the artist.

His grandfather was dead from the effects of coal dust on his lungs before he reached retirement age.

He felt her stir beside him, the golden girl, with Cambridge, the Riviera, the Louvre, the Uffizi to look forward to. In a few months she would have passed her driving test and would be able to take herself to the station. But from where he sat, he knew how often hope could be dashed or sidetracked. Maybe he was the lucky one, the silver boy, who could look back and cherry pick the past, keep all the precious moments (this would be one) and let the disappointments go without another thought. The young could travel round the world in hope and expectation, but with no guarantee of enlightenment, pleasure or peace. It was so much easier for an old man to sit with a glass of single malt in a half-lit room and remember.

The cat jumped down, restless, the sound of his paws on the polished floor unnaturally loud. The apple core she had placed on the table had started to discolour, to the pale amber of single malt.

"Come on," he said. "It's time we were making a move."

Her Mother's Eyes

Steven B Williams

"DO YOU KNOW WHAT TONIGHT IS, JOHN? It's ten years since you killed me."

There on the bed he stirs. The cold clink of metal startles. His awareness expands. A chain biting at his left arm tethers him to the wall behind. He tries to move his legs, but shackles bind him.

"Who are you?" he croaks, searching the dark, "Why are you doing this?" He cannot see her face but the decaying wedding dress she wears strikes him as a familiar lacery. "Is that... ?"

"John, you wound me." She steps into the glare of moonlight that stabs through the high windows and pools upon the hardwood floor. "You don't recognise your own wife?"

Her eyes. Those shattered blue eyes.

"Deborah?" All living breath threatens to leave him. "Oh God!"

She laughs. "God won't help you now, John."

"I SAID: Put it down!"

The man's hands thrust forward and close around the woman's neck.

She tries to free herself by beating her attacker across the head with the phone in her hands, but after landing a glancing blow, her fingers spasm and the phone clatters to the floor.

Her hands claw at the man's face but he tilts his head back – so, by virtue of his being taller, she cannot reach.

Blood vessels in her eyes burst. She can see flame-

84

wreathed stars crowding out life, and behind them the endless
dark that always waits.

"NO, YOU'RE D-D-D—"

"M-m-murdered." There's a shotgun over the woman's arm and the shadows dripping down the walls behind her meld with her raven hair to create a grim, broiling crown.

She comes to stand at the foot of the bed. The face of the woman he fell in love with so many years ago stares back at him.

"But don't you think the real question is why?" The cool perfection of her beauty radiates, and it settles on him like a freezing ash.

"Why then?" John blurts when the silence is just too much. "Why are you here?"

She takes a moment to answer, enjoying his agony. "It's time, John. Time for Justice. And here we are: Your judge. Your jury." She holds John in her acid gaze. "And you know what comes next."

"No! You can't do this. I never…"

A LITTLE GIRL left alone in the bath, the water tepid, the suds all gone.

She worries her mother will be angry if she tries to get out on her own, but her skin is beginning to wrinkle and her teeth are starting to chatter. No, there's nothing else for it, she'll have to rescue herself.

A towel waits on the rail by the door. She stretches for it and when at last she has managed to tease it down from its crook, she drapes it over her shoulders like it is a robe and she is a princess about to go to court.

On opening the bathroom door, a plume of dry air envelops her, bringing with it a wall of sound. She stands, a finger of caution playing on her lips as she listens. Her parents are arguing again, she realises, but with a ferocity she hasn't heard before.

She crosses the landing to the top of the curving stairs. She sits. Gently, she shuffles down to the next step. The raging voices are clearer now but not yet distinct.

She descends to the next stair and then the next until she is five down and can see into the living room. The pale uprights of the staircase bannister allow her to peer in on her parents without the danger of being seen.

The room is in twilight, illuminated by the flickering of the television and the rose wash of a lamp on the sideboard which shares its glow with a note pad and a quaint rotary dial telephone.

Her mother sits on the sofa, her hands balled into blanched fists, her posture rigid. "By the time I'm through with you," the woman croaks, her eyes molten with fury as she turns to the girl's mannequin of a father, "you'll be lucky to have the shirt on your back, let alone this house."

He stands behind the sofa, drinking from a Scotch glass, and seems mildly irritated by this display. "Debs, calm down. Let's not say anything we'll regret, okay? I..."

"Say anything we'll regret?" She throws up her hands. "The only thing I regret is that I've let you make a fool out of me! Well, not any more. I want you out!"

He carries on like he hasn't heard. "I'll change. We can go to couples counselling like you wanted. I'll... I'll get her fired. I won't have to see her again, yeah?"

"You think that makes what you did better?" The girl's mother yells as she marches to the sideboard.

"What are you doing?" her father says.

"I'm calling my parents, that's what."

"No, you can't!" He grabs the woman's wrist. "Your mum knows Richard. If she says anything... you know what my boss is like."

She wrenches her arm free. "Well, she's not been able

to keep a secret for the past 56 years. I can't see her starting now, can you?" Pleased with her delivery, Deborah picks up the phone and starts to spin out a number.

The girl's father bares his teeth.

"LET ME GO!" he rages, still trying to rattle himself free. "You've got it wrong. I've never killed anyone."

The woman in the mouldering wedding dress turns. Those cobalt blue eyes look back at him, unwavering and ferocious. The candlelight pulses. She slants her head down, and her high cheekbones catch the light to widen her joy. "Oh my! You really haven't figured it out yet, have you?" she coos as she slinks along the border of the room's shadows so her body, carved up by moonlight, becomes a diorama of pointed angles, "Alice saw you."

"I SAID put it down!" John's hands close around Deborah's neck.

Deborah, trying to free herself from John's grasp, beats him across the head with the phone receiver, but this only serves to make him more savage. John's lips pull back to show the pink of his gums. Saliva drips from his pointed tongue, splattering his wife's face and chest. After a second blow to his head, John wrenches Deborah to the side and the phone slips from her grasp, clattering to the floor.

Though Alice can no longer see her mother's face, she can still hear the woman's muffled screams, shrieks that intensify as Alice's father shakes Deborah's body back and forth, again and again, wringing her of all her warm life.

But eventually, when her mother's wheezing has stopped and the woman's stillness is absolute, Alice's father seems to become unsettled by the calm. As if waking from a narcotic sleep, he looks around the room, taking in the scene.

The upturned sideboard, the phone and lamp tangled on the floor, and the television, which had been on some news programme before, now a house of gnawing static.

John's gaze settles on the dead woman in his hands. He lets out a low moan.

The terrible stillness in the room devours yet more time until, weeping over his wife's body, John lays Deborah down upon the floor in the patch of light created by the overturned and now naked lamp. He begins to arrange the woman's limbs with a queer care so that, from Alice's partial view, it could be that her mother is just sleeping.

Then John stands and, in turning away from the scene so he can retch up his liquid evening meal, he accidentally nudges the body with his foot, causing it to uncurl itself.

Her mother's mouth, bruised as though stained with beetroot, has settled into an unnaturally wide maw. A livid scarlet has overtaken one of Deborah's eyes, the other a more terrible black, changing a shared iris into a glassy obsidian mirror that, as Alice stares, seems to devour everything.

Alice can't look away. She can't even scream.

"NO. IT WAS an accident. She wouldn't stop. She wouldn't listen and I... " John howls. "I'm sorry... "

The woman strokes her halved shotgun like she is coddling a snake. "What are you sorry for, exactly?"

"For *it*. For doing what I did."

"You mean murder." She bends down, resting her arms on the bed's metal frame so that she can look at him directly. "Murder. Say it."

"No, I can't." He shakes his head. "Please don't make me."

"Say it!"

"No. I won't."

A loud click. The two halves of the shotgun are now one.

He stares back at her, swallowing down his bile. "I *murdered* her."

She lets this settle. "You know, if you were really sorry, you could have turned yourself in."

"No. You see, I had responsibilities. A child to bring up. My job."

"Don't lie. You covered it up for you and you alone. But all that fear, all that hatred," she runs a hand over her breasts and down the flat of her stomach, moaning as she goes, "Oh, it penetrated your little girl, John. It changed her."

"YOU'RE SURE?" Alice's father asks the female police officer.

"We are satisfied that it was an accident, yes."

"I see." Alice's father looks to the floor, as anyone might if they were overcome. They stand in the exact spot in the living room where John committed murder.

"How did you find her?" Alice asks, her little voice chiming louder than it should.

John has a hold on his daughter's hand. Now he squeezes.

The female officer kneels before Alice. The woman is pretty, with skin the colour of rich chocolate milk. The round glasses she wears soften her angular face. "A man on a bike happened to look into the river. He was passing by on his way to work, you see. He saw... ." She thinks very carefully about how to term this next piece of information. "He saw that God made your mummy's arm lift into the light. The man said it looked like she was waving him down so that he could call for help."

Alice can see herself reflected in the woman's glasses. "You're wrong. She's still here. Mum's still here!" She twists free. She runs to hide.

"Alice, that's enough!" John barks, offering his hand to help the female officer rise. He directs her toward the door with apologetic haste. "I'm so sorry about her."

"Please don't be. Some children have a harder time

with this than others." The officer reaches into her pocket and takes out a small white card. "This is me. If you want the number of a bereavement counsellor for Alice, or have any problems at all, you just call."

John gives his most charming grin. "I will. Thank you."

Alice peeps out from her hiding place behind the sofa. Her father is alone now, leaning against the wall. His chest rises and falls. He gulps down air. As the moment softens, his attention turns to Alice.

"What was that about?"

She doesn't reply. John strides across the room and, taking Alice by her hair, drags her into the open.

"Well?" He kneels down and clamps her shoulders in a crushing hold. "I'm waiting!"

Alice does not speak.

Her father slaps her, and then it happens: as Alice's hair falls away from her stinging face and her gentle eyes fill with hurt, John recognises in his daughter something that he, in all his scarce attention and frequent absences, has never once absorbed about his little girl. She has her mother's eyes. This takes a hold of his heart – and twists. "Go to your room. Now!"

"HELP!" JOHN screams, testing to breaking the power his voice.

"They can't hear you." She moves to the window and looks out on the empty street. The night is so still. "And even if they could, would they come?"

From John's angle the woman casts no reflection. "People here love me," he says.

She turns. "You sent your child away, John." There is but a crack of silver light leaking through the curtains. It manages to mock him by picking out the loveliness of the woman's face. "That's something people notice."

"No, she *wanted* to go. I remember."

The woman stares back at him, this is a pronouncement she cannot deny.

"YOU'LL LOVE your new school. And your grandmother will like you being there. She needs the company. I mean, I'd move her in with us but you know we've never really got on. I'm too much like my dad, she says." John smiles, his hands gliding across the leather steering-wheel, the familiar scenery of home rapidly dissolving as they put mile upon mile behind them.

Alice's resemblance to her mother is ripening every day, both naturally and by cultivation. She delivers just one look, and John forgets to breathe. Seconds stretch until his lungs force him to suck in their fill of air. "I'll come and see you when I can. Some weekends, and then in the holidays," he offers, hoping this will loosen the spell.

They enter the womb of a tunnel, and the sound of the droning traffic above drowns out all else. With her gaslight eyes closed, Alice can feel herself drift, torn from the world and free to suckle on the teat of oblivion. It is filling her with purpose. She will live to hurt. To hurt him.

As the end of the tunnel nears and lights bloom, Alice returns her gaze to the world. John has driven off the main road, she notices, and they are close to the river. She looks to John. He has his eyes fixed on the road ahead and seems unaware of his error.

"This is where they pulled Mum out, isn't it?"

John flinches. He presses his foot to the car's accelerator.

"A new start for both of us," he cranks out with false cheer. "That's what we need. A new start."

She hears nothing after that. It's a simple idea but its effect is profound. A new start? Could her hollowness be filled? Away from him, could life begin again?

91

Seconds blink in and out of being. A field of resistance enfolds her. What little is left of Alice rallies in a sudden flurry of hope. Perhaps...

"I MEANT what I said. I *would* have visited." There is spite in his voice now, his fear settling like a caustic snow. "I didn't get a chance to, though, did I?"

Suddenly diminutive, the woman pulls her hands up to her chest as if in the precursor to prayer. "She couldn't risk hurting her grandmother."

"What are you talking about? Hurting her?"

"It's about inevitability, John." She draws out one long breath. "It doesn't matter what she wanted, how much she 'loved' her grandmother, how much she cared. Eventually her grandmother would have suffered. Alice would have hurt her."

She tiptoes across the room, passing the table on which she has placed a gathering of candles. The aura it casts gives her ivory frame a melancholy tinge of warmth, as though she is a frosted leaf caught in the early morning light. "Knowing that, how could she stay?"

ALICE'S GRANDMOTHER is there to greet her as she descends the small wooden staircase into the country-home kitchen. Alice has been in residence just a few weeks but the kindness her grandmother has shown her has been like a salve. Slowly, Alice is coming back to herself.

"Did you know the community fair is next week?" her grandmother says, sitting down at the breakfast table with a book in her hand.

"No," Alice replies, seating herself next to the well-preserved pensioner and shaking out some cornflakes into a bowl. She douses them – sparingly please! – with milk.

"Yes. We'd take your father down all the time when he was little." Her grandmother moves to take a sip of tea before

returning to the book in her hands. A brown leather book with gold print, the length of the average male's forearm. It is, in fact, a photo album. "I remember," she says wistfully. "John was such a demanding boy. Cross him and he had a mean streak. Look at this." With trembling hands she hands a folio to Alice. "We were at the beach. What beach, I can't remember. We ended up having to go home. Your father started screaming something rotten when the rain came down. Everything had to happen his way or no way at all."

Alice glances at the photo with only a cursory eye. The brown wash of a beach. The grey surf. A threatening dark sky run through with a glare of red.

Then her eyes fix on the little boy. She doesn't mean to look this close but she cannot help it. He wears the burden of a wool coat, thick and tight. John's unremarkable father, her grandfather, stands behind, a quelling hand on John's shoulder. Still, in this photo John seems happy enough. He seems...

She wrenches the photo album from her grandmother's hands.

"Alice, really! Be careful with that."

She tears through page after cellophane-wrapped page. Every photo of John shows the same thing, the same truth, until she can look no more and, shrieking, she throws the photo album to the floor.

Trembling, Alice makes her way toward the mirror over the hearth. She pits hope against all evidence that it isn't true.

What she sees in the mirror makes her scream.

Her grandmother, down on the floor and still trying to rescue her treasured memories, reaches out a hand for her granddaughter. "Alice, what the devil is wrong?"

"He's here! No! Don't touch me!" Alice shrinks back from her grandmother's touch. There is a second where it seems there is possibility. Her grandmother could lurch

forward and pull her granddaughter into a loving embrace.
She could still strip away the layers of hurt. But, for whatever
reason, she does not. And it makes all the difference.

Alice runs barefoot from the house. The wild hills of
the bleak countryside imbibe her. She will never return to her
grandmother's cottage, or the deceit of hope, again.

"DID YOU even look for your daughter, John?" A flicker in
the woman's voice like the afterglow of a filament.

John grits his teeth. "She died a few months ago. My
mother, I mean. Not that *you* care."

"*Not that you care*," the woman repeats back to him
in an empty, mechanical way.

The strangeness of this makes him falter. Finally, he
tries to divert. "God, what happened to you?"

Her head turns on her neck without her body moving
even an inch. The woman is no longer fragile or small
looking. In the half-light it would be easy to mistake her for a
living blade. "God!" she laughs. "You happened, John, like
you always do."

THE MAN'S body rolls over her like a sour wave lapping the
shore. He stinks of beer and sweat, and his unbridled gut
presses her into the gravestone at her back, making it hard for
her to breathe.

By day she sleeps in churches, chapels, and
abandoned country ruins. By night, with the sky above so
clear and the vastness of space nude and harsh, she lets men
rush against her in graveyards; sometimes for money,
sometimes in the hope that she will get lucky and one of them
will end her.

But they never do, and so she is left to whittle away at
herself under the ministry of crumbling stone angels.

"What's your name?" this particular drunk croaks in
her ear. News of a funeral tempted her out of hiding and now

94

she is here, doing what she does best.

"Debs," she replies, listening to the money jangle in his pocket like the beat of a special kind of heart.

The drunk folds her hair back from her face, perhaps to gaze into her blue eyes, perhaps to kiss her lips. She tries to turn away. "Come on," he puffs, taking a hold of her jaw to force the issue, "You've got a lovely smile. Let's see it."

She stares at him. Midnight becomes pitch and something inside her breaks. What was one becomes two, and neither is the little girl of so long ago.

Her hand searches the ground at her side, eventually falling on a bit of stone – a broken angel's wing perhaps. She picks it up and, in one swift motion, brings the rock down upon the man's head. She rolls the limp drunk away, allowing him to slump to the floor. She regards the stone in her hands with a keen pleasure, listening as it thirsts for a different, more deserving target.

SHE TURNS the stone over in her hand, the blood from John's head-wound still fresh enough to glisten in the low candlelight.

"You little whore."

This earns him a cobra's gaze. The quiet in the room gathers before her kerosene voice bursts: "Alone, day on day... week on week... year on year!" Screaming, she runs from out the dark and slams the rock into the side of John's face. Bone shatters, tissue caves. She skips away, cackling.

"But you're here now," John coughs. "Just untie me and I can..."

"What, so you can kill again?"

"No, I would never do that."

"Be honest for once! If you thought you could get away with it, you'd kill over and over..."

"No."

"...and over and over and over, and you would love it.

95

Because," she employs a giddy rush toward the bed, "it makes you feel powerful. It makes you strong. Oh, it just feels so good. Doesn't it, John?" She tiptoes around to him so she can press her forehead to his. "But look, you're chained up. You're powerless." Her breath is so warm it parches his broken skin. "Now I forget," and she feigns being coy, "do you like being weak?"

His glare turns white-hot. "What do you want, you little bitch?"

"Ah, there!" she sings. "We knew you'd come out to play eventually." She takes up the shotgun again and drags it across the wall above his head, making a fissure in the paper that disconnects all above from that which is below.

"Is it money? Do you want me to pay you to keep quiet? Fine! Just name your price."

Her joy is musical; one long note of stricken, throbbing steel. "Oh, you *are* going to pay, John. But not with money."

"Then what?"

When the woman has drawn out a full tour of the room, she sits herself at the foot of John's bed. She crosses her elegant legs. The torn wedding dress she wears falls in such a way that on show now is her onion white thigh and the frill of her garter. There, a glimmer of silver twinkles as she levels at him: "We told you. Justice."

IT'S HALF-SIX in the morning and the woman is waiting to begin.

The stolen car she sits in, a battered old two-door with an engine that sounds like it could rattle loose at any moment, splutters against the chill of the early morning's winter frost. Despite this, she is not worried about being seen.

Indeed, when John, unblemished by the steam train of time, comes out of the house in his pressed suit, sipping his morning coffee from a flask, he reacts exactly as she knew he would: he looks the car's way for a second before letting his eyes skip over to the expanse of road behind. The affectation of poverty makes her invisible.

John slips into his own car, last year's must-have red sports model, and he speeds away without a second glance to the wreck parked down the street. When the roar of John's desperately overpowered vehicle fades, the not-yet-woman lets her own car die. It will never start again, she knows, but this was always a one-way trip.

Snatching up the arm-length bag from the car's passenger seat, she steps out of the vehicle and, with her overcoat flying out behind her, she walks up to John's house and straight across the front lawn, marching down the narrow path between the exterior wall and the wood fence that skirts round to the back of the house.

At the house's rear door she removes her coat, revealing the stained wedding dress beneath. She wraps the coat around her hand and punches her bound fist through the small glass panel in the door. Having made sure the glass is adequately cleared, she threads through her naked arm. The latch is within easy reach and it turns with a satisfying click. With the door open, she waits just a moment. No alarm sounds. Discarding the trench coat, she enters the house.

The kitchen is different of course, homely wood turned to dull chrome, and the living room likewise redecorated with overtly masculine blues. She pours herself a whisky from the decanter on the sideboard and then sips her way up the stairs.

She is busy contemplating the fresh coat of beige paint on the walls when an intruding clamour from a room down the hall makes her pause.

She turns. When the sound refuses to die, she approaches the room. After a moment's hesitation, she tests the door handle. It groans, having not moved in an age. The door refuses to give. She searches and eventually finds the painted-over disk beneath the door handle that hides a keyhole. The sound, like a flock of birds taking flight, reprises.

Kneeling, she pries aside the lid hiding the keyhole and peers through into the room. Is there a light on? It is so bright she thinks there must be, yet from the backyard she saw no evidence to suggest this.

Something darts across the room in a blur of crimson black. She cranes this way and that, trying for a glimpse of the figure. She catches the curve of a limb, the fringe of a cloying shadow; it's a woman, but a full view is always just out of reach. Then the light intensifies and with thawing eyes she pulls her gaze away.

The disc drops over the keyhole. She stands and backs away down the hall. With this, all is quiet again.

Her hand goes to the black bag she has carried with her since leaving the car. It is time.

"NOW, YOU have a choice." She strokes his face. "Have the decency to kill yourself or *we'll* kill you."

John's arm surges forward with a cold crack, the chain pulling tight as he tries to grab for her. She has placed herself just beyond his reach. Her laughter rises like acrid smoke as, finally, he deflates.

"All right, let's make this easier for you." She stands and walks around to the foot of the bed. Once there, she holds out the shotgun by the barrel and shakes it. It is his to take.

He doesn't move.

"Come on John. What's it going to be?"

Seconds ripple by. A nerve in his jaw twitches. His breathing quickens. His hands flex in his lap once, twice – then John snatches for the gun.

"Free me!" he shouts, his fingers sliding to the shotgun's trigger like a clitoris to maul. In his desperation he no longer cares why she would allow this. "Don't think I won't shoot you, Alice!"

98

"Alice doesn't live here any more, John. There's only the dead now." Her glee returns. "And soon you'll be among them."

He roars and pulls the trigger – only for his flesh and bone to fragment in a nimbus of bile and blood.

Through the ringing silence of the aftermath, she comes forth. "Did you think we would give you a working gun, John? That we would do all this just to hand you an easy way out?"

He tries to curse her, but half his jaw is missing and what remains will only loll and flap. His right eye is a pit, his left an incarnadine well.

Yet just enough vision persists that he can watch as the woman, his daughter, his wife, cradles his broken, hollow face in her hands.

"Look at me, John." She puts her face inches from the remnants of his. "Do you understand how you damned yourself? How all that you are and all that you did brought us to this?"

She kisses his forehead. John dies trying to scream.

The woman lets John's husk of a body fall limp to the bed.

The sound of beating wings fills the air now and there in the candlelight she sways with that mighty sound. Growing wilder, her dance more frenetic, she begins knocking over candles with long sweeps of her arms.

The curtains catch fire. The bed ignites. As the inferno rises, she moves to her final act. From beneath her skirts she takes out a slip of a silver pistol that, hidden in her garter and pressed into her thigh for so long, has left a bruise.

She holds the gun in her hands like a bouquet of flowers, and she starts a slow walk out of John's smoke-filled bedroom toward the room down the hall; a room in which a little girl called Alice once slept and played.

As the woman nears the door, which to her mind now

stands open and bathed in a golden shine, she raises the pistol to her lips and kisses the cold metal.

All that remains is one simple task. She must wipe from off her face her father's smile.

Growing Pains

Sue Featherstone

BRRRR... JACK FROST HAS BEEN BUSY painting pretty pictures on the window overlooking my desk. I wish Jack had stayed home. If it's cold enough for him to be making his presence felt, the portable electric heater sitting at my feet will never belt out enough heat to raise the temperature even fractionally above corpse cold.

Perhaps Fr John was wrong? Evil-doers won't be consumed by flames but turned to ice in an everlasting freeze.

"Don't be silly, Philomena," Daddy said, when I suggested as much to him. "You haven't lived long enough to do anything really wicked." And, no, he wouldn't spend money on expensive draught-proofing or a better heater. "Put another sweater on," he said.

You'll note, I hope, that I carefully haven't described this place as an office. That would be far too grand a title for a wooden shed, with a felt roof and walls that can barely withstand a summer breeze, let alone a full frontal attack by the winds currently blowing in from Siberia.

"It's all we can afford," Daddy said. I'd agree, except that you'd think a man whose work van carried the logo *Sean Burke: Master Builder* could knock up something a bit more weather-proof without breaking the bank.

He could. But he won't.

Why? "Because there's nothing wrong with that old shed."

Of course.

He'd change his tune though if he had to sit here like I do, day in, day out, freezing my socks off. All three pairs of them.

"Oh no, I wouldn't ," he said. "You're living the life of Riley in that comfy lodge. You should be out here with me trowelling cement."

Lodge? Lodge? If he tried to sell customers a lodge like mine, he'd be sued for misrepresentation.

But all arguments fall on deaf ears. Daddy was brought up in the school of waste not, want not, and there was no way on God's earth he'd replace that shed while the wooden slats still held the roof in place. I'm working on that though – at least once a day I give the walls a hefty kick. More on days like today because it's the only way to get a bit of feeling back into my toes.

I tried to get Mammy to intervene. She's good at getting Daddy to do things he doesn't want to do – but no.

"No?" I queried, waggling my blue fingers in front of her nose. She brushed them aside.

"Think of it as good practice for when you lock yourself away in that blasted nunnery. Your shed will be a palace by comparison."

She doesn't approve of my vocation. Thinks it's a phase and I'll grow out of it.

"I thought all Catholic mothers wanted at least one son or daughter to join the religious?"

"Only the ones with their heads in the clouds," she snapped.

Bet she wouldn't say that to their faces.

She's wrong. Well, maybe not wrong about some mothers having their heads in the clouds. But wrong about my vocation. And once I turn 18 – only a year-and-a-half to go – I'll be taking the veil. Whatever she and Daddy may say.

"Phut," Mammy said. "You'll never last five minutes in a house of prayer."

102

"I will!"

She raised her eyebrows. "Really? And what about mass last Sunday? How many times did I have to nudge you and our Coleen to stop whispering?"

Coleen's my cousin. We're practically the same age and hang about together. Especially on Sundays when, apart from mass, there's not much else to do

"That was Coleen, not me."

"Six of one and half a dozen of the other," Mammy said.

"But mass is so boring."

"And there won't be a lot of masses in a convent?"

"It'll be different."

"Yes," Mammy said. "You won't have me nudging you to shut up."

Perhaps she had a point? A life of almost non-stop kneeling and praying might be just a teeny bit dull. I mean, once you've said one Hail Mary…

It's all academic anyway: the convent won't take novitiates under the age of 18, by which time I'll be properly grown-up and much better at keeping still. In the meantime, I'm making the best of a bad job and concentrating on supporting Daddy. He's a jobbing brickie-cum-plasterer-cum plumber-cum-general-odd-job-man. Jack of all trades, Mammy calls him.

"And master of all of them," he says.

It's true – he's very clever with his hands and he built the business up from scratch when he wasn't much older than I am now. "Didn't have much choice," he said once. "No blacks. No dogs. No Irish. The only one who'd employ me was me."

He's done quite well since then though and has a large and loyal customer base, mostly among other members of the Irish Catholic community in which we live here in Leeds. That's why right now, a couple of weeks before

103

Christmas, he's putting the finishing touches to a bathroom extension for Fr John.

And, when he's done that, Mr Maguire, the parish treasurer, wants him to put in a new bathroom at his house too. He'd like it doing before Christmas, but, sadly, he hasn't a prayer. Daddy's a good builder but he's not a miracle worker. Mr Maguire will have to wait until the New Year when Mrs Donnelly, who runs the school PTA, also wants her outhouse turning into a new bathroom.

Right now, bathrooms are big business.

Initially, I was supposed to be giving Daddy a hand to sort out his paperwork and invoicing because I'm good at sums and have what Mammy calls a "tidy mind". Daddy doesn't – unless he's on a building site when he knows exactly where everything should go. But at home, and in his office – a loose use of the term if ever there was one – he's practically clueless and, after a particularly stressful meeting with his accountant, decided he needed a bit of help. Me.

I'm good at it too. There's something very satisfying about restoring order from chaos and Daddy's invoicing and accounting was nothing if not chaotic. I started the Monday after the summer exams finished. It was a bit daunting at first – Daddy's idea of filing was to chuck everything into an old biscuit tin in the bottom drawer and say a prayer his accountant could sort out everything at the end of the tax year. So far, Mr Michaels has kept him on the right side of the taxman, but he told me it had been touch and go last time.

He came over on my first day and went over the basics of double entry bookkeeping. I'd assumed it must be incredibly complicated but actually it's reasonably straightforward. And Mr Michaels explained it really well.

"Don't hesitate to give me a call if you get stuck," he said. "No charge," he added. "If you can get the hang of this, you'll save me hours and hours of work at the end of the year.

And you'll be worth your weight in gold to your Daddy. Save him a small fortune too."

Slightly to my surprise, I liked working with Daddy, and the sheer variety of the work meant no two days were ever the same. So, though technically my job is still to just look after the paperwork and invoicing, my responsibilities have expanded quite considerably. This morning alone I've cycled over to Mrs Donnelly with brochures for baths and basins – and talked her out of buying an avocado suite; spoken on the telephone to the supplier to order bricks and cement; prepared a stack of invoices; and had a rather difficult telephone conversation with Mr Maguire, who seemed to think his status as parish treasurer didn't require a cash deposit before Daddy went on site.

After a fairly sharp exchange of opinions, he no longer labours under that delusion.

"I don't think you're being very respectful, young lady," he said when I reminded him – politely – about our pre-agreed terms and conditions.

Some of Daddy's customers, especially those who've known me since I was a small child, sometimes forget I'm a working woman now and no longer a schoolgirl.

"I'm sorry, Mr Maguire, but we've already offered a generous discount."

"Discount?" he interrupted. "Discount? You call knocking a few bob off for an old family friend a generous discount?"

"Yes," I said. "We do."

Long pause.

"Well, *I* don't," he said eventually.

"I'm sorry," I replied, "but if you feel you can get a better price elsewhere…"

He knew darn well he couldn't.

"I'm not saying I'm not happy with what you're charging," he said.

"No?"

"But I do think it's a bit much expecting money up front."

"It's customary," I said.

No doubt he thinks I'm a bossy, disrespectful hussy – he was muttering something to that effect as he hung up – but too bad.

And now, it's back on my bike to cycle to the presbytery to ask Daddy to stop off at Miss Mitchell's on his way home for lunch to change a bathroom light bulb. She's a canny old lady who used to be the local midwife and, in the absence of a husband of her own, relies on Daddy to do what she calls "man jobs". We have a lot of customers like her who expect freebies and, fair enough, changing a light bulb is a customer-service-loss-leader sort of job, but she keeps dropping hints about a leaky veranda roof.

If she thinks she's getting that mended for nothing, she can think again.

THE CYCLE ride warmed me up a little. It was one of those lovely, crisp glad-to-be-alive days you sometimes get at this time of year. "I'll miss days like this when I'm a nun," I thought. And the joys of vanquishing opponents like Mr Maguire.

Message delivered, I popped next door, into church to say hello to Mary and Joseph who are waiting for the arrival of the Christ child in a ramshackle wooden shed that's not dissimilar to my own.

Dipping my fingers into the holy water font, I made the sign of the cross and, genuflecting, slipped into a rear pew and drank in the atmosphere. You can almost touch the stillness. Who wouldn't want more of this?

Pity Sunday Mass lacked this magic. The spirituality seemed to fly out the door with the first long-drawn-out chords from the organ, invariably played at a funereal pace by our choirmaster's wife. Dear God! We could get through mass in half the time if she just moved her fingers a bit faster.

Sometimes it's not just Mammy who wonders if I'm cut out for being a nun. It's an honour and a privilege that God wants me to dedicate my life to Him but sometimes I wish he'd picked someone else.

But that's not really the right attitude so I say a quick Hail Mary and an Our Father and hope for the best.

Almost before I'd finished, the church door banged and a young man came in. I've seen him at Mass a few times. Mammy says he's Fr John's nephew. "Straight off the boat." By that she means he has recently arrived from Ireland.

"Another funny one," she said, giving me one of her looks. "Thinks God has called him too."

For someone who purports to be a devout Catholic, Mammy is very intolerant towards those inclined towards the religious life.

His name is Brendan McConnell. "Too good-looking for a priest," Mammy said.

I don't agree. Much better a good-looking priest saying Mass than an old fat one with boozy breath like Fr John.

Brendan hesitated at the door. I know Fr John worries about him and thinks he's too shy and lacking in confidence to be a successful priest. He'd confided in Mammy – people often do. I think they find her acerbic tongue a breath of fresh air.

They should try living with it.

The young man's family also disapprove of his vocation and sent him to England in the hope that six months with Fr John would be a wake-up call. Why does someone his age allow his family to boss him around so much? I don't have much choice – I'm not 17 yet. But *he's* quite old, at least 24 or 25. I shan't be at Mammy's beck and call when I'm *his* age. "No," says a little voice in my head. "You'll be answering to your Mother Superior."

Will that be any better? I know what Mammy would say.

Mammy had advised Fr John to turn off the central heating and to tell his housekeeper to serve lumpy porridge for breakfast and fatty mutton for dinner. "And no hot water for baths," she added. "Give him a taste of the simple life."

Daddy thought it was a hoot. "Perhaps we should send Philomena to join the young man at the presbytery," he suggested. "Sooner she gets used to plain fare the better."

This was unkind. I'm one of those long skinny types with empty legs.

"I'm a growing girl," I said. "I can't help it if I'm always starving hungry."

"They won't feed you as well as I do in your nunnery," Mammy warned.

"I'll be grown-up by then," I said, "and won't need as much food."

"It's to be hoped not," she said.

Fr John hadn't yet reported back on whether the plan was working but I thought the young man looked troubled. I sympathised. It's not easy hanging on to your vocation when everyone around you implies you're a God-struck idiot.

Brendan dipped his fingers in the holy water and gave a polite half wave as he walked purposefully towards the altar. He was dressed fashionably in a pair of denim jeans and a black leather jacket – rather like The Fonz from the new television sitcom, *Happy Days*. Impossible not to admire his rear view.

Should a nun-in-waiting have such thoughts? No prizes for guessing what Mammy would say.

Brendan knelt at the rail and, making an elaborate sign of the cross, bent his head in prayer. But he'd barely had time to say more than half a Hail Mary when he jumped up as if he'd been hit with a bolt from heaven. He glanced back at me. "Did you hear that?"

Yes, no mistaking the wail of a frightened baby. It was almost too clichéd – huddled in the straw-strewn manger and wrapped in a towel, the smallest baby I'd ever seen.

The towel was wet and stained with blood and something sticky and thick and greenish black.

"Meconium," Brendan said.

"Meconium?"

"Baby's first poop," he said.

I pulled a face.

He laughed and lifted the baby and unwrapped the towel. The umbilical cord was still attached. "He's not very old," Brendan said.

He looked healthy, though there were little creases of dried blood in the folds of skin around his neck and on his body.

"What do we do?" I asked.

"Take him to the presbytery," Brendan said, "and call an ambulance." He held out his arms. "Here, you take him while I see if the mother has left a note."

It was the first time I'd even seen a new-born baby, let alone *held* one. "You're beautiful," I whispered, kissing his little wrinkled forehead. He gave a faint mewing sound. "Do you think he's hungry?"

Brendan shook his head. "We'd know if he was. He'd be making enough noise to wake the dead." He'd finished stirring the now damp straw. "Nothing," he said. "Come on," he cupped a hand under my elbow, "we'll get some clean towels and give him a rub down while we wait for help."

I made a make-shift nappy with a tea-towel and a clothes peg and rocked the baby, now swaddled in an old dressing gown "borrowed" from the hanger on the back of Fr John's bedroom door.

"He's a grand little fellow," Brendan said, kneeling to tickle the baby's fingers.

"Makes you think," I said.

"Yes," he agreed.

THE BABY was taken to a nearby hospital. We weren't allowed to visit but Fr John told us the doctors were happy with his condition. His mother was eventually tracked down – a young girl of 17, only a little older than me, who'd just arrived from Ireland and was living with a sister. She'd hidden her pregnancy under baggy clothes, and eventually gave birth alone in a public toilet.

I felt so sorry for her. Sister Anne's attempts to address the facts of life on our last day at school had been very embarrassing, and confusing too, but I'd grasped enough to gather the mother must have been absolutely desperate to even consider giving away her darling baby. She'd tried two other churches before walking into ours, the first that was unlocked.

Fr John said the doctors thought she must have left the baby 15 minutes or so before we found him. Any longer and ...it doesn't bear thinking about.

I know some people thought she should have been sent to prison – but I was glad when I heard the police had decided prosecuting her would serve no useful purpose.

Sadly, we never found out what happened to the baby, whether he was adopted or returned to his mother. I hope so.

But I feel blessed that Brendan and I found him.

And each other.

Points of Convergence

Linda Jones

Adapted from *Searching for Breakfast*, a short poem by
Michael Jenkinson

SHEFFIELD, SUNDAY AND SNOW was never a good combination, especially at 10.30 in the morning. All Dan wanted was a quick escape route, to put some distance between him and the smothering blanket of emotion that threatened to swamp him. But her bed had felt so good and the taste of her...

Slinging the strap of his guitar case over a shoulder, he thrust cooling hands deep into jacket pockets and tried to concentrate on avoiding the icy patches.

A slate grey sky glowered between a patchwork of buildings; already more snow was falling.

Memory filtered back as he walked. The gig. In yet another dark space, flickering lights, surrounded by four band-mates as they sang out the old and new... mostly covers, from the late seventies and eighties. Springsteen, Bowie... but a gig was a gig and every pound he made edged him closer to that American holiday. San Diego and Comic-Con beckoned. And the place felt like a throwback, the old songs sitting easily with the flaking paint and brick walls.

Jay, the band's founder, way back in the dim and distant eighties, had pegged him for three lead vocals, which was a bonus. It must mean they'd at last forgiven him for being only 23. But that third song – where the hell had the man dredged that up? The dark ages?

There had been the usual nerves, the buzz of anticipation. A growling fizz of noise as bodies piled into the venue.

111

Injected with alcohol-fuelled enthusiasm, the dance floor was soon swallowed up under a tapestry of skin. There had been a tang of damp wood, swiftly coated with the scent of human sweat, a heady combination.

Jay and Ian often reeled off stories of their earlier years, where the air had been so thick with the haze and stink of tobacco, you couldn't see further than the edge of the stage, but not anymore; the place had been crystal clear.

Until *she'd* walked into the room.

Dan hummed the melody, bringing back that first image of glowing skin, black hair caught in braids, and those eyes. At first the song had been just another meaningless lyric. He'd sort of heard Ian's tirade during rehearsals, about the Young Rascals and their under-appreciated brilliance.

But Jay and Ian were always going off on one: diving into the past, searching for lost treasures or maybe just happier times.

Ian had been so right this time. The rhythm and flow of the music suited Dan's voice.

As the first chords of the keyboard filtered out across the room, the unusual quality of the melody had been enough to lift more than a few heads and eyes. The crowd were used to the battering, up-beat rhythm of early rock; *this* was 60's in the raw.

"How can I be sure in a world that's constantly changing...?" And there he'd stood, centre stage. For once the audience were silent, the intensity of the moment terrifyingly brilliant.

She'd walked through the doorway just as he'd started to sing, her eyes immediately latching onto his. Everything else had faded.

"Whenever I'm away from you I wanna die because I wanna stay with you..." He'd sung to her, for her...

The applause at the end had been deafening – frightening. For a moment he'd hardly known where he was. And then

112

she'd been there, leaning up with those deep eyes of dark chocolate.

The rest of the evening had disappeared in a blur of fast-paced music and him constantly searching for her face in the audience.

At the end they'd come together. She, moving in careless grace, caught his hand. "Come home with me," she'd whispered. Outside, pressed against a poster proclaiming *60's music rocks* he'd kissed her for the first time and started to sink.

The cold night had melded into a whirl of senses. Touch, taste, the smell of her, every nerve in his body tingling with expectation. They'd half fallen up the narrow stairs to her flat. Tumbling into soft sheets, he'd murmured her name "Shala," and he'd clung onto the sound like a lifebelt.

When morning came, there'd been no lurch into consciousness, no guilty pangs as he'd woken to a new day. His arm lay wrapped warmly about her waist and she was smiling.

SOMETHING RATTLED under his boot, bringing him back to the cold street. He looked down between the folds of scarf at an empty carton, the scarlet stripes vivid against the snowy surface. It was just the usual rubbish ditched after a Saturday night.

Dan shrugged his guitar further onto his shoulder and glanced around, suddenly not sure where he was. He'd been down this street a few times before, or so he thought, but the edges of white blurred the memory, confusing the map in his head.

A door on his left opened, releasing a cloud of steam and the welcoming aroma of cooking eggs and mushrooms. He could have sworn the cafe hadn't been there the last time he'd walked down the road. A duffel-coated figure shuffled out of the café, grunted something, as Dan obligingly stepped to the side. He'd go in, grab a sandwich. There'd be nothing to eat in the flat when he got back.

Inside, seven tables were spread with red and white check plastic, surrounded by 30 black vinyl seats and only a couple were free. The place was buzzing. A long counter ran across the back, with a couple of high black-topped stools standing guard.

From the open kitchen Dan caught the sizzle of bacon, the chef's spatula clanging against the edge of the grill. On the wall, dozens of posters pouted or smiled down; a young Elvis Presley, Dusty Springfield, James Brown... He was still taking in the captured images when a gruff voice interrupted,

"So what's it to be? We do a great breakfast omelette..." and the bald headed chef thrust a blue menu sheet into his hands.

"Yeah, that sounds good and a coffee, please," Dan reached for his wallet.

"Were you doing a gig last night?" The chef was looking at the guitar case by his leg.

"Yeah, up at Rock Cavern. Do you know it?"

"I know Frank, the owner. He's ploughed just about everything he's got getting that place up and running. So you can put that away, lad. Have this one on me." And before Dan could say a word, the man had turned, yelling orders to the red-headed kid in the back. "One breakfast omelette, large, and a coffee...."

Sliding into a seat, Dan let the conversation around him seep inside his head, mostly about football, and the astonishing fact that both Wednesday and United had managed a win. No wonder the mood in the place was so cheerful.

He pulled out his mobile, but there wasn't a hint of a signal. The weather must be really bad. His coffee arrived first; white-mugged and strong enough to start a jet engine. As he sipped, beginning to enjoy the bitter taste, his gaze wandered to the artwork on the facing wall. A young Aretha Franklin stared back, but those eyes... they were all Shala. He couldn't look away.

"Would you like any sauce, mustard maybe...?" The bald chef was there, sliding a large plate onto the table in front of him.

It was all Dan could do to drag his eyes back. "No. And thanks, I really appreciate this."

"You're welcome and maybe next time you're back at Frank's place, I'll get to hear you sing..." and the man was gone, back to the steam and noise of the kitchen.

The omelette was packed with mushrooms and a great tasting cheese and all the while, as Dan ate, thoughts of Shala and their night together played in his head.

It had never been like this. Before, he'd just add a phone number to his mobile, knowing he would never ring. He'd walk away with some guilt but never this sense of loss – regret, if that's what this strange ache really was.

The door to the café opened, letting in a blast of arctic air. A woman hurried in, stamping flakes from scarf and knee-high boots. "Freezing out there," she declared to no-one in particular.

Reluctantly, Dan finished his coffee. It was time to go before the buses decided not to run. Walking four miles in a blizzard wouldn't be fun and no way was he paying for a taxi, not on a Sunday. With a wave to the chef and the room in general, he stepped outside and into the biting cold.

HE'D WALKED down a couple of streets, turned yet another corner, before he realised he had no idea where he was. There was no-one around, not even the usual cars straddling the kerb.

Perhaps he should go back, ask at the café, but the snow was falling thick and fast. Better to keep walking, reach a main road. There was bound to be something he recognised soon. Or a bus stop. Anything to give him an idea of direction. He'd crunched his way a few more yards when a young woman emerged from a dark doorway on the opposite side of the street.

He shouted across: "Sorry! Can you tell me what road this is?" But she either didn't hear or didn't want to. Mini-skirted and scarfed, she tottered along the pavement to hammer on another door just a few feet away. A welcoming glow of light ushered her in before closing against the chill.

Dan shrugged and lifted the guitar onto his other shoulder, and only then noticed the small shop window. Set amongst the hodgepodge of two-ups and two-downs, it looked back at him, unassuming.

There were posters of 60's album covers pinned to the back wall: Beatles, Chuck Berry, Dusty Springfield, Elvis... And sitting amongst a scatter of vinyl singles were several guitars for sale, one that had his stomach lurching, his heart pumping. A Gibson Hummingbird.

The richness of the two-toned wood mocked him. How many gigs would he have to do to even raise the deposit? An icy wind seeped under the hood of his jacket, biting into his neck. Reluctantly he dragged his eyes away. One day…

The wind had picked up, whipping flakes into a frenzied dance and spinning something else that hit his cheek. He saw the flicker of blue paper as it fell to the pavement – two £5 notes? He stooped to pick them up only to frown at the touch. Even with cold fingers the texture felt weird and the image of the Queen was way too young.

Someone coughed, sighed. Dan twisted around, staring into the recess of the shop doorway. Under the large CLOSED sign, a pair of piercing grey eyes gazed back. The notes fell from Dan's fingers, forgotten. The eyes belonged to a doorway refugee. He was sitting, huddled up against the door, wrapped in an overlarge grey coat and woollen hat that had definitely seen better days. The eyes seemed ancient but they looked out from a face hardly more than 18, if that.

"Hell, you must be freezing!" Dan didn't think twice, just unwound his thick scarf and handed it over, hoping the lad could understand. The touch of the teenager's fingers on his was like ice.

"Thanks." The muttered reply was clear enough.

"There's a café just a couple of streets away." Taking out his wallet, Dan pulled out a £10 note "You need to get out of this weather..."

Ignoring the money in Dan's hand, the lad reached out to pick up the blue notes from the pavement and stared at them as if they were made of gold. "You're giving me all this? I can't thank you enough." He reached up to clasp Dan's hand with those freezing fingers. "I'm Archie Waterton... Only my dad died and the landlord threw me out... I came into town to try and find work, but... This is unbelievable." He was staring at the notes in his hand, as if they were going to disappear into thin air.

Dan shifted uncomfortably. "Okay..." The lad had to be sick, not right in the head if he thought a couple of dud £5 notes would solve the problem. With a sigh, he unfolded another two notes. The American holiday would have to wait a little bit longer.

"Look, take these as well just in case." And while Archie tucked the scarf around his neck, Dan slipped £30 into the pocket of the huge coat. "You *will* go and get something to eat, get some help?"

Archie smiled up, his eyes reflecting a glowing determination. "You don't waste chances like this, not ever. And I won't..."

Dan had walked to the end of the street when a black Morris Minor slid around the corner. He had the briefest impression of hands gripping a steering wheel hard; and dark, quiffed hair as the man tried to hold his course on the

117

untreated surface. He watched until the vehicle disappeared into another street, all the while hoping to see Archie walking away, but no shuffling figure appeared.

It was no good, he couldn't just leave him. If Archie stayed where he was, then he'd be reading about a dead body in the morning.

With a sigh, Dan turned round and called out into the driving snow as he walked: "Archie, how about we both go for a tea or a coffee, get out of this mess for a while?" But Dan was talking to himself. The doorway was empty.

"What the hell...!" It had to be the right place. He bent to scoop up the £30 that now lay on the floor. The notes were already partly covered with flakes. He sheltered his eyes, trying to see more clearly through the white. There was only one set of footprints tracking away: *his*. Dan turned to the doorway. Archie must have gone into the building. The sudden chill that shivered up and down his back had nothing to do with the icy wind.

The CLOSED sign had disappeared and across the bottom of the door was a thick line of snow and ice sealing the door to the step. That door hadn't opened for hours or days most likely. There wasn't even a scuff mark to show where the teenager had sat.

This was too weird. Dan reached for his mobile. He needed to hold something solid, to hear a voice, anything to ground him. But there was nothing; no signal, no life. He stared at the blank screen, not sure if it was panic or fear that was creeping into his stomach. He needed to get out, move. It had just been some weird guy – a strange coincidence? Shrugging further into the hood of his coat, he tried not to miss the comfort of his woollen scarf.

From above his head came a squeak of wood against brick, a window, opening. He stepped off the kerb to gaze up, but flakes fell thick and fast into his eyes, blinding him. Music pumped into the street, heady, tinny. It took a moment to work out what he was hearing. "Sweets for my sweet, sugar for my honey..." The Searchers and, by the sound of the recording, it was a really early one. A young voice was singing along, not exactly in tune.

He yelled up, hoping to make himself heard over the noise. "Hey! Excuse me! Can you tell me which street this is?" Like it had never been, the music just stopped. No-one answered.

Irritated, tired and more than a bit freaked out, Dan leant his guitar against the wall and dug inside his jacket to pull up the collar of his shirt. Anything to try for some warmth. And only then noticed the shop window.

Where the Gibson Hummingbird had stood only minutes ago, was now a boarded up window. Stark blue, orange and red graffiti swore back at him. Monstrous. Impossible. He grabbed his guitar, backing away; this was a trick, someone was playing mind games... He'd seen it. Every single detail of that instrument was burnt into his brain. He hammered on the wood hard enough to hurt. It was real enough.

He was almost running, feet slipping under him as he retraced his steps. The café would still be open. It couldn't have been more than a quarter of an hour since he'd left, tops. He checked every doorway as he went, half expecting, half hoping to see Archie grinning back at him.

But the end of the third street came and the café was nowhere to be seen. How could the place not exist? He'd followed his own boot prints back, hadn't crossed any other roads...

Without much hope, Dan fumbled for his mobile. When the screen lit up and the signal icon flashed, he punched the air with relief. He pressed for the last number he'd rung; Shala's. He'd put her on before he'd left... And a sudden, awful wave of fear hit him in the gut. What if she wasn't real? What if...?

He leant his head against cold brick, counting down the seconds... "Be real, you'd better bloody be real..."

"Dan ... is that you?"

"Oh God! Shala? I couldn't find my way out of the place. Nothing's sodding real."

"Hey, it's okay. Are you hurt? Where are you?"

"Not a bloody clue! Seriously, I stopped in a café a few streets from you but I can't even find that now."

"What café? The nearest is miles away in town. Never mind that now. Can you see a street name?" She was calm, patient, "Most are high up on the wall. I've got an A to Z right here, so just find a name."

Dan lifted his eyes, searching. Directly opposite he caught sight of the black lettering. "I think it says Midland Street only I'm not..."

"You are kidding, right?" she was laughing. "Turn around and look up..."

Black braids were swinging through an open window. "It looks like you found your way back to me. I'll buzz you up."

She was waiting at the top of the stairs, dark eyes smiling in welcome. "I'm glad you came back."

He slid out of his coat and into the kiss as though everything in between had been nothing more than a dream.

It sounded even crazier when he told her, but she listened, as they lay together in the crumpled sheets, content, soothed.

"Maybe there's a new café opened up. A 60's theme," she suggested. "We could do with one this end of the city and it does sound really cool." She frowned thoughtfully, idly running a soft finger over his chest. "But I don't get why that name, Waterton, is so familiar."

The music on the radio faded, the local news bulletin filling the space. There were the usual reports of crime, accidents, along with snow drifts and cancellations, nothing new, until...

"And finally, the death has been announced of Sir Archie Waterton, civil engineer and benefactor of several homeless charities and housing projects in Yorkshire. He died peacefully at home this morning, aged 71. Made homeless at 17, he often talked about that terrible day when, penniless, he'd travelled into the city to search for work and ended up huddled in a doorway, freezing to death. Several others, who were homeless at the time, lost their lives during that horrendous winter of '63. He always stated that if hadn't been for a stranger's generosity that day, he would definitely have been one of them..."

Beside him, Shala shivered and moved closer into Dan's side, "Please stay. At least for tonight."

As Dan gazed down into those dark eyes, the icy tendrils of dread melted away. Archie had been right: you didn't give up on chances like this. "I've never met anyone like you, Shala. I'm not going anywhere and that's a promise."

The Box

Susan McCartney

THE WOODEN TRUNK MATERIALISED in the doorway of the Fair Care Charity shop on the Pontefract Road. Its extraordinary carvings sizzled through the mist of the early morning. Olive, a volunteer, didn't see it.

"Ouch!" She rubbed her shins. "Who left this here? Nearly went me length."

"Ey up," said Elsie. "Don't know, love. It wasn't there when I opened up."

"Help me get it in then." Huffing and puffing, they dragged it through.

"The box is smashing. It could make a few bob on its own," said Elsie, running fingers over the peculiar carvings of mythical creatures. A five-toed dragon covered the lid; its tail, holding a fan, coiled around a golden lock. The dragon's eye held her gaze and she gasped as it morphed into a galaxy of stars.

Elsie shook herself. But Olive never noticed, as she was busy raking through the contents. With a wince, she struggled up, holding a dress of silk, lace, and shining beads.

"Take a gander at this. Proper 1920's vintage this and a make. This'll do well."

Elsie admired a biscuit barrel. "Victorian and hand-painted, I'd say. Is it a leprechaun peeking from behind them red spotty toadstools?"

Olive squinted. "Can't make it out but I'll see better when I get my cataracts done." Olive pulled out what appeared to be a diving suit. She sneezed as she shook off the dust. "Flippin eck! What's this? Looks like one of them old ones with a goldfish bowl on top"

Elsie glared like a vulture laying an egg. "And straight out of one of them science fiction films from the 50's," she said with a giggle.

Olive shrugged. "Maybe someone will buy it for fancy dress but I can't see anybody using it for real."

Elsie grinned, showing large false teeth. "I know. We'll make it a feature, put a silly hat on the helmet and some fairy lights. It's amazing what you can sell." Elsie pulled out a small bronze cat. "Look at this, it reminds me of Fluffy. I miss her that much since she passed. I'd buy it but it'd be too dear. It's got them *higher-ogliffix* things on like real antiques." A lump in Elsie's throat threatened to choke her. Her eyes filled with tears and one dripped from her nose but she brushed it away, hoping Olive didn't notice.

Olive squeezed Elsie's shoulders. "The charity won't mind if you buy it. We'll see what price they suggest and we might be able to get it between us."

Elsie gave a little smile. "It looks like she would have guarded a Pharaoh's tomb. Never mind, what else have we got then?" With a grimace and creaking of stiff joints, she pulled out a pair of men's patent dancing shoes.

Olive held them up to the light and sighed. "These could've come off the feet of Fred Astaire. Bobby dazzlers these – perfect for a smooch with Richard Gere."

"In our dreams, girl. What else have we got?"

"All sorts. It's like Christmas Day when we were kids – opening presents and feeling that prickle of excitement."

"Yuch," said Elsie, "Don't like this creepy painting."

Olive took it and squinted at the oil of a mansion and graveyard. "Nor me. Is that a skellington in the corner or a shadow? I can't see a bleeding thing these days." She peered through yellow fog. "There's a signature. *Goya* or somebody?"

Elsie snorted. "I thought that were a scent."

123

Olive laughed. "This box is odd. The more we pull out, the more there's left in." She ran dusty fingers through fine white hair. "I'm fair flaggin. Mash some tea, our Elsie?" But she forgot the tea and began to rummage again. She studied the painting with its macabre scene and shuddered. "Let's hang the horrible thing on the back wall. It fair gives me the willies!" She gave a cry of pleasure as she hauled out a pair of vintage sunglasses.

"They'd suit your face a treat," said Elsie.

"Sun glasses! My eyes need bottle bottoms these days! Mind you, they're smashing. I'll put a pound in the till for now. That's more than enough for a pair of glasses from the Ark."

"More than enough, Olive. Now let's have a cuppa before we finish unpacking that box of tricks."

They had just time to wash the pots before the doorbell tinkled with their first customer of the day.

A CARE-WORN woman stood before them, looking like she was wondering what she was doing in the shop at all. She reached in her pocket and found a coin that she didn't know she had.

THE BISCUIT BARREL

KATE RUSHED through the door of their house and caught her mother off-guard. "Forgot my phone," said Kate. The words froze on her lips as she saw the wreck that was her mother.

Sandra looked up in shock, eyes swollen and red. Tears and snot crusted her eyelashes, ran down her cheeks and stained her sleeves. A letter fell from her hand as she brushed an arm across her face.

The words broke free. "Mam! What's the matter?" Kate said, running, stumbling towards the stricken woman and grasping her by the shoulders.

The sobs continued in staccato hiccups. Sandra gasped: "I'm fine. It's nothing. A dose of the *poor me*, that's all." She sniffed and tried to stem the tears.

"What's this?" Kate picked up the letter. Sandra tried to snatch it but Kate was quicker. It didn't take her long to get the gist. She sank to the floor and exhaled a sigh of shock and anger. "Mam, the bank says they're foreclosing on the mortgage. This can't be right." She ran her hands through her hair, "We've never missed a payment."

The sobs grew to a crescendo as Sandra lost control and rocked backwards and forwards, tears dripping from her chin. Kate cradled her like a baby. Words staggered out. "I'm so sorry, Kate. Our savings are gone. Lost my job... couldn't tell you... too ashamed."

"But...but..." Kate held her mother's face, looking into her eyes. "You went to work every day with your briefcase."

Drawing a breath, Sandra shook her head. "They let me go months ago. I didn't fit in with the new personnel strategy at 50. Too old, you see." She almost managed a smile.

"Where did you go every morning?" Kate's eyes held fast.

Sandra squared her shoulders. "I went to the library to e-mail CVs and to work on my book. Had sandwiches in the park and met some interesting people, mostly unemployed like me. I'm writing their stories. *And* mine."

Kate's eyes grew wide. "Stories! You're writing a book?" Reality came back like a drenching in iced water. Kate took charge. "We'll make an appointment with the bank to see if we can just pay the interest." She shrugged. "I guess it's a rain check for the holiday with the girls."

Kate scowled at the cluttered room. "We could sell your collectables on E-bay. You being such a clutter bug." She brightened. "It won't be the first time we haven't had a pot to piss in since Dad left. And we managed before."

"Sorry love, should've told you before." Sandra sighed. "A banana's got more backbone. I could do with a drink though. Gin?"

"Strong coffee on its way." The kettle whistled, cups rattled and the air was filled with the smell of Arabica beans as Kate came back with two steaming mugs. "What's that by the sink? What junk have you been buying now?"

"Oh, the Leprechaun Cookie Jar? Who could resist him for a pound? His little face made me smile." Sandra sipped her coffee. "Went in the shop to get out of the rain and before I knew it, he was wrapped."

Kate flourished a £5 note. "Did you know there was money in it?"

Sandra frowned. "Can't be – I washed it up and put in some custard creams." It occurred to Sandra that the money was Kate's.

Kate rose and grabbed her phone. "I'll nip back to the stall and ask Vince for more hours. Business has been good lately." She gave her mother a hard stare then softened. "Don't worry. I'll sort this out."

WHEN KATE got back from work, Sandra was busy at her computer. Stories burst from her fingers as they flew across the keys. Her eyes shone – gone was the haggard Sandra who came home each night from the college where she'd worked as a lecturer in Literature.

"Good news, Mam. Vince says I'll get the hours. Fancy a cuppa and a bickie?"

Hope was beginning to grow in small shoots. "That would be lovely."

As the kettle boiled, Kate reached for the biscuits. In the cookie jar was another fiver. She called out: "Mam, when we've had our coffee, I'll nip to the shop and get some veggies and mince. Fresh soup and spag bol for tea."

And so it went on. Small amounts of cash appeared in the cookie jar – just enough to tide them over. The bank agreed to give them some slack with the mortgage. They managed.

SIX WEEKS later, Kate threw off her shoes at the door and sighed. "Put the kettle on. I'm gasping. It's been hellish busy at work." She looked up to see Sandra smiling. "You look like the cat that got the cream cake and the canary."

"I put my book on the net and it's flying. I didn't want to say in case it flopped. The reviews are brilliant." Her grin turned into a full blown laugh. "And..."

Kate whooped. "And what else have you got to tell me?"

"I got a part-time job delivering creative writing at the University." Her eyes filled. "I'm not on the scrap heap – people want me."

They hugged. "I've got news too," Kate whispered. A smile threatened to break her face in half. "Vince is moving to a new shop in the arcade and he wants a manager. I guess that would be me."

Grasping each other by the arms, they danced around the room laughing and singing *Happy Days are Here Again*.

"Kate, I think it's going to be alright." Sandra flopped in a chair to catch her breath.

THAT EVENING they sat with feet up and a glass of wine. Each was thinking the same thing but Kate said it first.

"You know it was good of you to put spare cash in the cookie jar."

Sandra looked up frowning. "*I* didn't. I thought *you* did."

"No! You did! You've got to be kidding."

The women looked at each other and rushed to the kitchen.

Kate picked up the jar first. "The leprechaun, he's winking. But there's no money in it this time."

"You know what, love? It's because we don't need it now. We're through the worst."

Kate gawped. "A magic cookie jar – trust you to find it." She grinned. "Let's pass it on to Mrs Grey down the stairs. Her old man's lost his job. The cookie jar can cheer her up at least. You never know, it might work for her..."

"That's a smashing idea, love. Let's raise a glass to our little friend."

"What's Irish for *Cheers*?"

"Don't know. But I'm sure he won't mind."

THE DANCING SHOES

"YOU GET down here right now, Kevin Johnston, and stop hiding in the bathroom. Mandy will be here any minute. Grow a backbone, Kevin – it's only a dance."

He did as he was told. "Gran, it's a competition and Mandy's entered us. Told her I had all the moves, but she'll find out it was all lies and I've got two left feet, and an ironing board has more sense of rhythm."

"What you need, Kev, is the right shoes. Look at these – got them in the charity shop today. Lovely patent leather and dead light. Slip them on and we'll have a bit of tripping the light fantastic."

"It won't help, Gran. Mandy's never been the same since she saw that old film *Saturday Night Fever* on TV. And stupid me told her I could dance like that guy in the film."

"You *can* dance like that John Ravioli, our Kev. He's only wiggling his hips and throwing his bum and arms around."

"He's got hips like a snake and mine are like a hippo giving birth."

"That dancing's a doddle. Put them on and we'll have a bit of a practice before Mandy comes. I'll show you how we danced the Jitterbug."

He laughed – and for the moment his mood brightened. "Alright Gran, just to please you. Gimme the shoes. They feel dead nice, like I'm walking on air." Then Kev's feet decided *they* were in charge and twirled and whirled him around the little room. He sat down with a gasp. "Didn't know I had that in me. Bring it on, Mr John Ravioli – you can't hold a candle to Kev Johnston in his white suit."

Kevin was dancing an inferno when Mandy walked in and the look on her face said it all. Soon all three were swaying hips to the music of the Bee Gees.

THE VINTAGE DRESS

"I'M SORRY, Miss Parker, but there's nothing more we can do. Make your last few weeks count. Have a holiday and make memories."

"Thank you Doctor. You've been very kind. I'll do something special. There's an ad in the paper for a 1920's weekend at Goldthorpe Hall and I have just the dress. You'd never believe I got it in a charity shop. It's a real vintage find."

"Goldthorpe Hall – I thought that burnt down years ago? Maybe I'm mistaken."

"I guess so, Doctor. Or they wouldn't be putting adverts in the paper."

"Have a wonderful time, Miss Parker."

"I will, Doctor. I intend to make every day special."

SOME DAYS later a taxi dropped Pollyanna Parker outside the magnificent Art Deco front entrance of Goldthorpe Hall. She looked radiant in her Lanvin dress despite the illness that was consuming her. She squared frail shoulders and entered. Music of the jazz age poured from the ballroom. Her pinched face lit at the sight of the "bright young things" dancing the Charleston. Soon she'd be dancing with them. Then she saw him, the handsome man in the white tuxedo. Their eyes locked. Polly knew that, come the end of the evening, she would be in his arms and it would be heaven.

They danced cheek to cheek and Polly was enveloped in soft feathered wings that held her safe. She sighed and closed her eyes and together they ascended and she was in paradise.

THE PAINTING

ARNOLD FOSTER'S eyes glinted when he spotted the painting. It couldn't be! But yes, it was the real McCoy. He licked fleshy lips with a mouth that was suddenly dry. He had struck the Mother lode – surely a genuine Goya. Worth taking a chance at least!

As a dealer, Arnold made the rounds of the charity shops looking for antiques lost in the mountains of bric-a-brac and fusty clothing. If only the two old bats serving didn't know what they had! They looked as if they'd come down with the last shower – lambs to the slaughter. He put on the smile he kept for the gullible, his lack of interest feigned. The two old ducks smiled at the prospect of a customer.

"That painting. Is it for sale by any chance? It's a copy of course – no great value, but I have an interest in macabre art, no matter how modest and poorly executed."

130

Olive looked at Elsie and Elsie looked at Olive. The message passed between them – a buyer for that horrible painting!

Arnold almost ran from the shop but made himself slow down. The price! He had paid a fiver for what might be a Goya! Another day and another sucker suckered. Back at his mansion, he salivated over his booty. Pensioners were his speciality – handing over precious antiques for a pittance to supplement their pensions. He had "acquired" his new home in the same manner. A family of aristocrats down on their uppers had sold Arnold their stately home for a song. The owner had topped himself.

He examined the brush work. He was now sure it *was* genuine. In typical Goya fashion, the painting was eerie in the extreme. A skeleton striding towards a large country house that seemed very familiar. The creature's empty eye sockets glowed with malign intent.

"I thought that skeleton was hiding by the trees. No matter," he said to himself, "It's likely a trick of the light." In the morning he would take the painting to a Regent Street gallery. He smiled at the prospect of a real killing.

"COVER HIS face. It's giving me the horrors," Constable Jones shuddered.

Inspector Galway winced at the contorted body. "My impression would be the victim died of fright if it were not for his bruised neck. This is a rum one. There's no sign of forced entry so he likely let his murderer in. The pathologist should give us more to go on."

"I know it's a posh house but I wouldn't live here – not with that cemetery next door. The place fair gives me the creeps." Constable Jones frowned. A noise behind made them both jump.

"What's happened to my uncle?" said the young man with the weasel face.

"This is a crime scene, sir, and I must ask you to wait in the hall so you don't contaminate the evidence. We'll need to ask you a few questions."

The young man looked at the corpse with a speculative eye and left the room. Propped against the hall wall was a painting of the house and cemetery. Moments later it was stashed in his car. He returned to the house after putting on his serious face.

"I THOUGHT we sold that vintage dress, Olive."

"We did – to that pretty girl who looked so proper poorly."

"Well, it's back on the rails and like someone's been having a pillow fight with it. There's feathers stuck in the seams." Elsie frowned and turned to her friend. How's your eyes? Heard anything about your cataract op?"

"They say they've never seen anything like it. The cataracts have shrunk and it's dead queer. But I can see even better with my new sunglasses."

The bell tinkled as a customer entered. In no time at all, the "diving suit", now in a bin bag, left the shop with a puzzled customer to Olive's cheery wave and call: "That'll be champion for the Scarecrow Festival."

OLIVE GAVE Elsie a hug. "I phoned the office about a price for the cat statue. They said a couple of quid. Anyways, I bought it for you – my treat."

"Oh Olive, I'll treasure it – just like my Fluffy. My heart nearly broke when I saw it gone."

"Take her home, put her by your bed and say goodnight to her every night. Right then! Enough of this sentimental lark. We've a shop to run. Let's get cracking on this bottomless box."

The two ladies gave a joint groan as they knelt before the box for another rummage.

"Elsie, do you think young Colin is dumping donations into it rather than taking them round the back?"

"He says not. What've we got? *Love Potion Number 8* in a nice blue bottle. Here's a box of make-up that's brand new. A moth-eaten Teddy Bear and an old leather-bound book. This ruby necklace is nice – well ruby *glass*, I suppose."

Soon more items were dusted and displayed in the overstuffed little shop.

NIGHT FELL and the sun and the charity shop snored. The old box glowed in the moonlight and the air around it crackled and sparkled with specks of dancing fairy dust. It replenished.

THE NEXT day Elsie got busy dusting the bric-a-brac, giving Teddy Bear a quick hug. "I dreamed Fluffy was sleeping on the bed and when I stroked her, she purred. It was such a comfort. How's your eyes by the way?"

"I'm a bleeding medical marvel. I can see great. Think I'll apply for a job as a fighter pilot."

The doorbell tinkled and their first customer of the day stood before them looking a little confused. Her plain face lit up when she saw the blue glass bottle and its glowing contents.

THE PERFUME BOTTLE

THE CUSTOMER looked in a trance. *She's got a pretty face under those thick glasses*, thought Elsie, *but that suit does nothing for her*. Elsie knew a designer suit when she saw one. Elsie would have described the young woman as *Venus in a too tight skirt*.

Christine wondered what she was doing here. She'd only meant to pop out for a coffee but now thought it rude not to buy something. The two old ladies beamed with expectations. The blue glass scent bottle caught her eye, its contents winked. Unfastening the stopper, she took a tentative sniff. The scent was delicious – she gasped with pleasure. Her pulse raced.

"You alright, love? I thought for a second you were going to faint." Olive was holding the younger woman's arm with concern.

"Sorry, but that scent went straight to my head. I'll buy it – the bottle is so pretty." The designer bag opened and the scent bottle was wrapped in newspaper and popped inside.

Olive nudged Elsie and pointed an elbow to the make-up box. "Made just for you, love. Blue shadow would suit your violet eyes."

"But I don't wear make-up," said Christine. Her protest lost, another sale was in the bag to a perplexed customer.

"I'll pop it in with the scent bottle. Brand new. And what an unusual box!"

Christine looked at her watch and cried out in alarm. "I'm going to be late back and Mr Norwich will be worried. I'm always there and he's so kind to me." She clapped her hand across her mouth.

Her mobile rang. It was Nick. He spoke with no preliminaries. "Meet me outside your office when you finish. Bring some cash. I'm meeting some mates down the town. Make it a hundred and don't keep me waiting."

"Am I included?" Her voice was pleading, desperate.

"It's a *guy* thing Christine."

Tears prickled and she gulped them away. Olive and Elsie tried not to make their eavesdropping too obvious.

"Be there are six sharp and don't keep me waiting if you know what's good for you." The phone went dead. Before the two ladies could speak, Christine was out of the door, tears streaming.

134

"HAVE YOU been crying, Miss Purdy?" asked John Norwich, her boss of ten years.

"My hay fever, Mr Norwich."

He smiled. "We'll have a cup of tea. And once you're up to it, we can discuss the Finchley contract."

"Thank you, Mr Norwich. Is it alright if I leave before six today?"

"Are you meeting that young man of yours?"

She wondered if he had accented the word *young*. But he wouldn't. She was being over-sensitive but they both knew that Nick was 15 years younger.

Christine had convinced herself Nick loved her despite the things he said and did. The other night at Enrico's, she'd accused him of flirting with the waitress. He'd muttered: "Old bag thinks she's my mother." Just loud enough for the other diners to hear. She'd fled to the ladies. On her return, he was gone but the bill wasn't.

Biting her lip, she turned to the files. Without thinking, she opened her bag and took out her charity shop purchases. The blue glass bottle sparkled and before she knew it, *Love Potion No. 8* was dabbed on pulse points.

"You smell nice, Miss Purdy." John placed the Finchley file on her desk. He stared. "Could you use your keen legal mind and go over the contract's finer points, Christine? Sorry. *Miss Purdy*. Drop it on my desk once you've done. Enjoy your date tonight."

"Oh, I'm not going out tonight. Nick's got a date with the boys."

"I'll be back about six, Christine." He gave her a long look before picking up his coat and Panama. "It's Nick that's missing out."

Christine pulled out her mirror to see why John Norwich had been staring. Her nose was likely bright red to match her eyes, she thought. The idea of using the make-up box popped into her mind.

"Can't have Nick making jokes about my face," she said as she reached for the make-up box. Inside was a treasure trove of colours and aromas. Blue, mauve, and silver shadows sparkled and pink lipsticks whispered to her to try them. A powder brush beckoned and she dusted her nose. Her skin shimmered with light and youth. The powder was glitter free but her skin looked like it had been bathed in stardust. A dash of rose lipstick and her lips were plump and kissable. A stroke of the silver on her lids brought out the violet in her eyes. To her the mirror revealed her usual face but with a nose that no longer glowed.

Satisfied, Christine turned her attention to the Finchley contract and worked her magic on the intricacies of small print.

"SORRY CHRISTINE, *Miss Purdy*, I forgot the Jenner contract and it was necessary…" He gaped. "I must dash, Christine. See you before you leave." In a fluster, he was out and running to his car.

Christine turned to her in-tray. Time flew on skis and when she looked, it was gone six. Nick would be furious that she hadn't been to the cash machine. With only £25 in her purse, Christine prayed that it would do and he wouldn't be angry again.

NICK DIDN'T look up from his phone. He growled as she panted up behind him. "You've made me late, you stupid fat cow. She'll not wait."

His face contorted, fists bunched, he turned and looked at her. The phone fell but he didn't notice. He was transfixed, spellbound, the waitress forgotten. For the first time he was in love.

But Christine saw *him* for the first time with clear eyes: she saw the brute. He had been meeting a girl! She stepped back, repelled. Christine pushed him away and ran back in a panic.

"Please, Christine, please...!" he sobbed. But it was no use. Something had snapped in her brain and she was cured. He shambled off the office step and out of her life.

Christine was trying to make sense of it when John returned. She told him: "I've split up with Nick."

He took her hand. "Christine. Have *I* got a chance?"

"Oh yes, John." A thought popped into her mind. She ought to go back to the Charity shop and re-donate the perfume and make-up. They had done their magic and perhaps someone else could benefit. But when she looked at her desk, they were gone.

THE MYSTICAL chest shimmered in the moonlight. Its lid opened once as if to say goodbye and it vanished in a cloud of sparkling stars. Only Teddy Bear saw it leave. He waved a paw. Many miles and years later it re-materialised...

Hole in the Road

John Winter

WHY NOW? IT HAD BEEN OVER SIX YEARS since Ruby walked out on him, and now suddenly he couldn't stop thinking about her. A quick glimpse of a face in the reflection on Cooplands shop window had started it – Tom turned round quickly, scanned the crowd, but couldn't see her.

Last night he had fallen asleep at his desk, drunk, and woke up abruptly when a breath of air brushed across the hair on his neck. His stomach heaved, his head ached and so did his back, the result of sleeping across the desk.

His mates had gone home and left him in the Bankers Draft which, from previous experience, he knew was just a crawl from the newsroom at *The Sheffield Star* office in York Street. He had a vague plan to rest a while then get a taxi back to his flat on the Manor, but that didn't happen.

As he stood up and staggered towards the loos, he saw a figure in the dark corridor, a vague impression of long hair and a short skirt. Was it Ruby? No, nobody was there.

NEXT MORNING Tom didn't look too bad. He had managed a shave (keeping an electric razor in his desk drawer proved useful) and no-one appeared to have noticed he had on the same clothes as the previous day.

As he left the *Star* loading bay, he was greeted by Old Jack, one of the Commissionaires, who was going off duty. He said: "Saw you come in last night but you never left. Heavy night was it?"

"It was a bit. Keep it to yourself, will you Jack?"

"Of course," Jack chuckled.

"I think there was a woman in the office as well, wasn't there?"

"No, I didn't see anyone come in or go out. Nor did the monitors show anyone moving around. Maybe you dreamt it."

"Maybe," said Tom, but he knew he hadn't.

NEXT TIME Tom went into the Banker's Draft, the manager said: "You *are* one of those reporters, aren't you? At *The Star*?"

"Yep, and one of your best customers if you're thinking of giving us a free pint."

"I wasn't. I just wanted to tell you that we had two break-ins. Someone stole meat pies and bottles of beer. Might make a story for you."

"Might do. When was it?"

"About a month ago. And something else – Pat my deputy was locking up early this morning and there was a woman sitting on a stool in the upstairs bar. Pat watched her, just sitting there, waiting. Then the woman made off through the double doors to the front stairs but when Pat chased after the woman, she was gone, completely vanished. Not in the toilets or anywhere. Didn't go through the unlocked front door because Pat's husband was waiting for her there."

The last time Tom had seen Ruby they had been in the upstairs bar. They had a row over a Valentines card Tom had received from a girl in the office. It meant nothing. But he hadn't seen Ruby since. He had rung her mobile, left messages with her mum, but she never answered.

Tom was feeling depressed when he walked out of the front door of the Bankers on to Castle Square to get the tram home. Now the paper was printed overnight, there was no sense of urgency about his job any more, no rushing for deadlines, no holding the front page. He was bored, and he couldn't forget Ruby.

A woman ran across the pavement in front of him. She had long hair and a pale face, and large, sad eyes that looked straight into his. Ruby was beautiful, as always. She was gesturing with her right hand for him to follow.

Tom knew her at once, but he hesitated. "Wait, Ruby, why…?"

But Ruby carried on, urging Tom to follow,

Tom ran towards her, but was suddenly grabbed around the neck from behind and punched in the stomach. Two men dragged him, coughing and retching, into a dark alleyway and threw him on the ground. They took his wallet from his inside coat pocket and pulled out a credit card. "What's yer pin number?" snarled one.

Tom kicked out, catching the bigger hoodlum on the shin, and swung a punch at the man standing over him. The two men started kicking him. Even though he tried to roll away and cover his head, the blows got through. He blacked out.

A FISH was peering at him. Tom could hear the sound of water lapping, and a pump, and there was a bright light above. His face was reflected in glass, bruised eyes, bloody nose. Another fish swam past, larger, a carp. It was an aquarium, set in a blue curved wall, and he was sitting on the floor next to it, although it wasn't a floor but bare, cold concrete.

"Are you feeling well enough to sit up?" A man was slumped in a worn chair next to him. He looked old and tired, emaciated. "I'm sorry I can't help you up, I'm just too exhausted."

Tom sat up. They were in a small room, stretching back into the dark. A table, two chairs, two beds. A primus stove under a blackened area of the ceiling. There were a few rugs and coloured posters in one corner. The walls, such as they were, emerging from the shadows, had no logical shape;

almost as if piles of stone and concrete had been piled up and abandoned. The blue wall with the massive aquarium was the only suggestion of decoration.

"How did I get here?"

"I brought you here," said the old man. "We sent for you, and you came."

Tom stood up, the pain of his injured ribs catching his breath. "But I was being attacked. I was in Castle Square, and a gang beat and robbed me. Are you part of the gang?"

"No, of course not. I'm just an old man nearing the end. Ruby's lad helped. She was bringing you to us, but those men mugged you. The lad told me they had you so I went up there to help. With this gun." He pulled a shotgun out from under the rug that covered his legs. "They soon ran off."

"And you dragged me here?"

"Me and the lad – Ned. He's gone out looking for food. He's learning how to forage."

"But where are we?"

"Under the ground, of course. The Hole in the Road."

Tom shook his head in disbelief. "But that was filled in years ago, back in the 1990s."

The old man laughed. "Most of it was, but they left a bit. I was sleeping rough down here even while they worked. I left it too late one day and they filled it in. I scrambled around and found a hole, an air pocket maybe, and some gaps that led through to the basements of some shops and to the Bankers. We get in and out that way. I fitted up some lights, managed to get the aquarium working, and lived here ever since."

Tom remembered the Hole in the Road. It was a local landmark, a kind of sunken pedestrian precinct, the hub of a series of underpasses. The aquarium was incongruous, but fun. Otherwise it was a bleak place, where youths gathered and petty criminals plotted, the Hole in the Road gang for one. He shivered. "Why did you choose to live down here? It's pretty horrible."

141

"The police were after me, and there were people I owed money to. It's safe down here. I either found food or stole it from local shops, cafés. Ruby was sleeping rough, homeless and desperate. Thrown out by her parents. We kept each other company down here, and then Ned came along. She made things comfortable for us."

Tom gazed at the aquarium, the fish looking out, and saw his reflection next to the old man. And there, smiling back, was Ruby!

He turned round, joyful, desperate – but she wasn't there!

"What's happening!" he shouted. "I saw her, but she's gone."

The old man sighed. "She's always coming and going. About a month ago she fell ill with headaches and I made her go up and find a hospital. I didn't know what was wrong with her. And then I fell in the street and I would have been a gonna if Ned hadn't found me. We were in real trouble, and I knew Ruby had to bring you here. She always loved you, you know. It was difficult, but she and Ned had this sort of telepathy going. So we kept in touch with her. Now you have to take the lad and look after him, 'cos I can't."

"Why me?" Tom said. "Why can't Ruby, now she's better?"

"It has to be you," sighed the old man, "because Ned is your son and Ruby died two weeks ago."

The Honey Trap

Brian Lewis

I thought of Chatterton, the marvellous boy,
the sleepless Soul that perished in his pride.

I do what I always do – write the title and then write
towards it.
Know the permitted wordage and keep that in mind.
Don't write to the deadline, but if you have not started in
ten days,
then abandon the whole thing.
If you think of something like the above quote from
somewhere in the far recesses of your mind,
thrust it into the text and let it simmer .
Don't bother to Google. Googling is a distraction

THE APPOINTMENT OF PATRICA SUTTON as
Vice Chancellor of Hallam University came as a
surprise. Her husband's sudden death on the eve of his
investment ceremony was unfortunate; but, since
Sheffield is a city where sentiment quickly translates into
action, the decision to make his wife his successor was
both convenient and logical. The newspapers loved it.
Arthur had been Hallam's third Vice Chancellor; she
would be the fourth, also the first woman to hold the
office.

Arthur's death had been dramatic. Going for what he
called 'a leak in the dark', in the middle of the night, carrying a
box full of his last book, *An Alphabetical People's History of*

Sheffield, and pondering if the clocks went forward or back, he had mistook the last step for the tiled floor, turned right and hit the stair post. He then stumbled into an unnaturally high tower of boxes of books. The first box broke his neck, the next his shoulder and the third mercifully missed his foot by half an inch but left a bruise on his ankle.

Introduce the main character quickly and establish a key location that you know – in this case Sheffield.
Then invent a house. One in Ranby Road would be a good choice.
That is where artists and writers you know live.
Describe a situation which is just about feasible but ends on a tenterhook, a detail – such as the bruise on the ankle – which you might use later.

Disturbed by this catalogue of co-incidentals, the garden twine which was hooked over a single picture hook, which held the print *The Death of Chatterton,* broke; and the picture fell off the wall, crashed into a bronze Ming incense burner and sent a shard of glass diagonally towards Arthur where it severed his carotid artery and vocal chords.

Develop the main character's personality, quickly but do not bother to describe physical appearance.
Recognise that if this short story is to go anywhere significant,
it has to have an unusual format.
Do as I am doing now: suggest that the reader reads the main text
(Times New Roman, ranged left)
and then the Notes To The Potential Writer
(Arial, centred)

At the inquest, presided over by Coroner Wasp, Patricia, in a written statement, said that she slept through the initial commotion which must have followed the fall. She also said she thought she might have heard Arthur's final whimpers but she was not sure. The next door neighbour had an attention-seeking flat-faced French Bull Dog who was only silent when eating, and she thought that she heard what she described as "growling noises" but she was really first aware that the day had begun in an unusual way when she realised that Arthur, a creature of habit, was not beside her greeting the world with loud snores, a well-honed irritation. Otherwise the house was silent.

Here introduce something that happened to you or someone you know.
When my wife fell down the stairs and was screaming for help,
I did think that it was next-door's dog.
Use inverted commas to indicate importance as well as speech.

It then occurred to her that tonight was the night the clocks went back and, although it was more like 6am "new time" than 7am "yesterday's time", something was wrong.

To the question "When were you aware that something untoward had happened?" she replied: "As I searched for what I call my Papal slippers, Sir, I thought: *That is odd*. That my husband, as was his want, was wondering our home, making adjustments to Time. He and our son collect clocks. I then went onto the landing."

Always proof-read the text after it has been type-set.
Inexperienced authors, glad to see the back of a manuscript, celebrate and do not look for new errors.
Typesetters can discover what looks like a mistake but

wasn't, and modify the text. For instance, one might in the above paragraph alter the word "wondering" to the common-sense "wandering."

In this case the alteration seems justified until we see that the reliability of Patricia's spoken "witness statement" depends on "wondering about the house". Printers love this sort of mistake because it is usually picked up when the author sees the final proof and may create a need for extra or fewer pages. Printers make the money from these sorts of errors to send their children to private schools.

As she often did, having spoken a sentence, Patricia's mind turned a corner and she made a split-second analysis of what she had just said, disliked it but decided to press on. She was a world-renowned award-winning author and this quality of analysis was a significant part of her academic toolbox.

Good. We have further established the academic credentials cited in the opening sentences.

She felt that the key sentence just uttered had at least three problems. The first: Why had she used the archaism, *as was his want*?

She thought that this was the first time in her life she had used it; and concluded that, having addressed the coroner as Sir, she recognised that a constitutional feature of this Court rested on principles found in the Magna Carta, a written instrument of Medieval justice established in a well-known social context. Judicial authority is one of the three pillars of Modern Democracy. The other two – "The Passage of Statute Law via both Houses of Parliament" and the "Monarch's Prorogative" – are critical articles of the English Constitutional Process.

It is useful in an English murder mystery to cite defining moments in national history which account for the greatness found in Great Britain and relate to justice. No matter what continent children or their parents came from, they must know in addition the names of the wives of Henry VIII; the dates of the Battle of Hastings (1066), the Battle of Bosworth (1485), and the beheading of Charles I (1642). They must also know that fire broke out in Pudding Lane, London, in 1666, and about the Charge of the Light Brigade (mid-19th century) and the assassination of the Arch Duke Ferdinand in Sarajevo in 1914.

Of these, The Magna Carta, signed at Runnymede.(1215) is the most important. For it ensures that the fictional character in *The Honey Trap* and all of the Muslim taxi drivers you have ever asked "What is so good about their adopted country?" will answer: "We are all equal when it comes to the law."

These thoughts made her adjust her pattern of speech to suit the occasion. The phrase *As was his want* and *Sir*, though instinctive to a girl from Wakefield Girls Grammar School, was appropriate when addressing a Coroner, especially one who was educated at Sandhurst and also a Knight of the Realm.

SHIT!

Who said that?

Then there was the word *home*. Since the children had left their *home* in Ranby Road, she and Arthur rarely spoke to each other. Could this, their house, she asked herself, still be considered a *home*, with all the warmth that word implied? She then wondered if she had said *wondering* or *wandering*, when she addressed Coroner Wasp. Arthur, cerebral before all else, could well have been wondering about time, therefore had she expressed a deep felt belief that he was, as usual, being indecisive? Why had she said Arthur was going around, "Making adjustments to Time'" rather than "Putting the clocks back"?

BULL SHIT

Why do you have to interfere?

BECAUSE YOU'RE A POMPOUS BASTARD WHO'S SHOWING OFF.

We all know that. You tell me all the time.

THAT'S BECAUSE YOU *ARE*.

All writers, and painters for that matter, must be.

GET ON WITH THE TALE.

She was flustered. So, pulling herself together, she quietly repeated the evidence given in her written witness-statement but made minor adjustments, putting special emphasis on *wandering* and inserting the article *the* to make the sentence more conclusive. Looking the Coroner in the eye, she stood straight and said: "I thought, Sir, that my husband, as was his want, was wandering our home making adjustments to the Time." Then she paused, seeming to compose herself.

It is hard to settle back. When I check Tools (always a necessity if the length is prescribed) I see that I have 3342 words to go to the end of the narrative. The check to this point is 1510. At this point in our history Henry VIII had just married Katherine of Aragon.

148

LET'S NOT ARGUE.

Yes, put things to one side.

YES, THAT'S BETTER.

We have a deadline.

The pause was seen by Coroner Wasp, who – though married – was not very aware of womanly practice. He thought that the pause was significant and not the sort of response an academic woman, about to recall how she found her husband dead at the bottom of the stairs, would make when recalling her distress. She was acting a part. Her control was admirable, a stiff upper lip, English sort of thing, but not the whole story. He was right. It wasn't.

She went on. "When I realised that something might be wrong, I put on my house coat..." (Actually it was Arthur's old dressing gown.) "...and went onto the landing where I put on the hall light. We have a two-way switch and it can be operated from a point outside our dressing room and one by the front door. He lay spread-eagled below, clutching the frame of the *Death of Chatterton*."

The painting had been so long in the hallway that Patricia barely noticed it. But initially she was both attracted by Wallis's oil and discovered that her erstwhile friend, and more recent rival, Judith Lintern was too.

YOU ALWAYS WANT TO SHOW OFF AND TELL THE READER WHAT YOU KNOW. OFTEN THIS IS NOT WHAT IS NEEDED TO MOVE THE TALE ALONG. THIS IS A MURDER MYSTERY, NOT AN ACADEMIC THESIS. GET A LIFE

Sorry. It's a bad habit. I talk too much.

On hearing of Arthur's death, Judith had sent a home-made card signed *lots of love* and, not unthinkingly, *regards* or *sincerely*. The rift that occurred over a dead man she had on a couple of occasions seduced – in the interest of scientific enquiry and with his wife's permission – was healed, it seemed. On getting the card in which Patricia told her of Arthur's passing over and the inquest, Judith therefore decided to attend the Coroner's Court.

Patricia had noticed her enter and was not happy. Ever since the younger woman had bested her in the dispute over who wrote the "sexy bits" in Lawrence's *Lady Chatterley* – Frieda or DH Lawrence – she was always nervous in Judith's presence. She had let Judith use her sewing room and her day-bed in a piece of "action research" but now doubted the woman's integrity. On that occasion the younger woman had tied Arthur up and threatened to thrust a carved carrot up his bottom.

I LIKE DETAIL. THE FACT THAT THE CARROT IS CARVED SUGGESTS DELIBERATION AND URBANITY. ON THE OTHER HAND, THE COLLISION OF TWO COMMON NOUNS – CARROT AND BOTTOM, THE SECOND NOT EVEN A NOUN IN QUEEN'S ENGLISH TERMS, AND OF A DIFFERENT TONE – SEEMS CLUMSY.

I disagree. The image of an upright carrot colliding with such a common euphemism as "bottom" is fresh and funny.

THERE ARE ALTERNATIVES.

Arse?

THAT IS TOO PRECISE.

It also lacks a sense of fun. It is common. *Anus* is clinical.

ARTHUR WOULD NOT THINK IT SO.

How can you say that? He's a fictional character.

HE STILL HAS TO BE BELIEVABLE.

He knew the escape word, which modern lovers seem to need to have agreed on before underclothes exploration takes place.

ARE YOU SURE?

Look it up in *50 Shades Of Grey – The Concordance*.

SO WHAT WAS THE PASS WORD?

Haystacks.

NEVER!

It has to be a word that you do not use very often. It crops up in a D.H. Lawrence title of a short story.

Judith is a tad mad.

***TAD MAD* IS GOOD. RHYME USUALLY IS, IF NOT OVERDONE IN AN "UNDERMILKWOODY" SORT OF WAY.**

That is too clever by half for me.

NO-ONE IS PERFECT.

Judith had a ruthless streak in her, though deep down she was kindly. But if that episode leaked out in this court, Patricia was done for. She knew the victim well, too well. In the taxi over, she wondered if it was normal for ex-lovers to think well of the dead and decided that it was. The sexual things – such as the poor timing and his leaving off when she had barely started – was common enough, only a part of the relationship. She thought of the laughs they had after the episode in the Barnsley hotel, when he, stark naked, reckoning to be a priest, had sat listening to her confession in a large wardrobe – which had once been a confessional – made her smile. The words carved over its door were *Pax vobiscum, Peace Be With You*. Very apposite today.

As she entered quietly and settled in the visitors' gallery, an usher in white gloves placed the image of Wallis's *Death of Chatterton* on an easel. The print was twice the size of the original and was called Exhibit B. She had assumed that the shard of glass which had severed his carotid artery was Exhibit B. As he lifted it into place, the Court Usher held it 'portrait' not 'landscape' and in that orientation she saw not the long dead poet lying on his death-bed, one arm extended towards the vial of laudanum on the floor, but the image of Christ, his right hand still pinned to the cross piece of the Christian Cross as disciples led by Joseph of Arimathea supported the body prior to withdrawing the final nail. It was powerful.

THAT'S A LONG SENTENCE

Yes. Cut. Agreed.

Judith was the only black woman in the court room that morning and she entered as if she was the Queen of Sheba. Gone were the black tights, sensible skirt and denim top of the Attercliffe Middle School teacher. In their place was a recently purchased pink, white and emerald green suit which owed a serious debt to Mary Quant and Bridget Riley. Around her neck was a torc of Yoruba gold. In the dock, Patricia, standing up straight with her hands at her side, signalled that she had seen her by raising one finger into the horizontal. Judith stroked the side of her nose in response for – though in academic terms they were sworn enemies – they really liked each other.

From the time they had first met and talked in the tea room of Sheffield Art Gallery about intuition, and Patricia had given Judith permission to give Arthur a sexual overhaul in the interests of her Action Research project, they were inseparable. Or, to use a term from early adolescence, "best friends". They were no longer this. Disputed ownership of the resultant book was the sticking point.

YOU HAVE ADDED ANOTHER 901 WORDS TO THE TEXT. YOU HAVE ALSO PUSHED THE STORY ON IN A PROVOCATIVE WAY WITH THE MINIMUM OF DETAIL. WE NOW HAVE THE ENTRANCE OF A KEY CHARACTER AND THE POSSIBILITY OF SEXUAL INTRIGUE. THIS IS A FUNDAMENTAL IN AN ENGLISH MURDER MYSTERY.

There are exceptions, for instance *Sherlock Holmes*.

As Judith sat down, the Coroner was asking Patricia why the pile of boxes was inordinately high and got the answer that the deceased, in the optimism of a wannabe-self-publishing-best-selling author, had over-ordered the books. They were in a pile that reached to the picture rail. "Three metres, M'Lord. In a very narrow hallway." was what she said.

Probably Guilty was what Coroner Wasp wrote on the case-notes.

When she had opened the house door two days before the death to an urgent knock and found Mr Akbar standing there, she said: "Yes?" And he responded, in a home grown Yorkshire accent, with: "Where would Madame like these precious commodities?"

The back of his van was open and inside were rows of two-feet-square boxes reaching up to the roof. Her first thought was that Arthur had ordered thousands of copies of his newly written Sheffield history book. It was paid for with Arts Council South Yorkshire money matched by a Sheffield Council grant, via the department he still Chaired.

Although it was a bit out of character, Arthur was both scrupulous in his integrity and stingy as far as money was concerned. He had been odd for a week or two and very odd in his dealings with her. She put this down to his recognition that his academic honours were, to her way of thinking, trumping her journalist ones. These days the bulk of her work was with the *Reader's Digest* and not with the *New Yorker* or the *London Review of Books*.

He had stopped loving and wanting her. However, it was mutual because all the love she had for him had disappeared. When most partners swopped lovers, she did not – out of loyalty to him and to the children.

He bored her. Night after night, party after party, he repeated the same anecdotes and only became silent watching Julie Christie make love on videos they hired from Block Buster. Once, when she tried to tell him about one of her successes as a journalist, he had shut her up with "Shush! I'm listening to the Shipping Forecast."

As far as loving was concerned, his time was up. But what should she do about it?

And then it happened. As she bent forward to sign the receipt which Mr Akbar was offering to her, her nipples responded by hardening. She guessed that he was looking at her cleavage and was well pleased. Her breasts, though petite, often suggested the way forward. Her mind was a brake, her nipples and imagination were not. He was young and fresh and handsome.

At that point it had not been her intention to kill Arthur, just inconvenience him. But as she began to be slightly damp, she thought that murder was on the cards. How the deed would take place was anyone's guess. She had read enough Agatha Christie and Reginald Hill to know that most anything could become a weapon of destruction if you had determination and followed your heart.

THE PHRASE "I COULD MURDER HIM" IS COMMON ENOUGH. IT IS NOT NECESSARILY GENDER-BASED BUT I TEND TO THINK OF IT AS WORKING CLASS FEM-SPEAK.

You cannot say that anymore. It is not PC, nor is it statistically correct. There is no longer a meaningful class system any more.

WE ARE ALL IN THIS TOGETHER.

Sort of.

WHEN SHE HAD STOOD WATCHING HIM BLEED TO DEATH, SHE COULD HAVE PHONED.

I suppose she could.

WHO WOULD HAVE THOUGHT THE OLD MAN HAD SO MUCH BLOOD IN HIM?

Possibly. Do you have a Shakespeare tag for
everything?

The boxes were stacked high because Patricia immediately fancied young Mr Akbar. She told him that the pile of boxes should stand two abreast near to the bottom of the stairs. She went down into the cellar for their painting steps. When she came back, he had brought nine boxes into the entrance. The tenth was propping the door open. He said: "There are 22 boxes. I will place them here, go park the van somewhere where there are no yellow lines and, like the Jhinn in the bottle, return in a trice." On that he bowed and was gone.

He was beautiful. Her grandmother's generation had been overawed by Rudolph Valentino and the silent movies. *The Sheikh*, the sands of the desert and the fullest of full moons, captivated them. Her mother favoured the American musical: Bing Crosby and *High Society*, queer dancing sailors and seven brothers leaping over chairs to get to sisters dressed in gingham, but not her.

YOU CAN'T SAY "QUEER" ANY MORE.

But what if I mean "odd"?

BEST NOT USE IT IN A BOOK.

She wasn't going there. Nor was she interested in singing nuns and Audrey Hepburn with a cod-Cockney accent. Sally Bowles, Edith Piaf and Joan Baez were important to her but not as important as Amitabh Bachachan, the greatest of all Bollywood stars. The dignified Indian constraint, so powerful and stylistic. There was no kissing, just a girl in a sari holding a flower and making it slowly rise until it came to a full-stop at 45 degrees close to her breasts. Pow. Mega Pow.

She looked into the delivery man Akbar's eyes and saw there a quiver of the uncertain hormones of early manhood and mixed in the scrummage and erotic eclecticism which her Nana had no doubt experienced with the Sheikh in the 1920s. The mix of male dominance, sexual slavery, dark men on white horses was lethal, a far greater turn-on than the books of Raymond Chandler. Akbar disturbed her. She was a bit flummoxed by the reference to the gin in the bottle, but let it be. If they ever needed a bed-talk moment that would be a good start.

She was especially turned on by Akbar's bottom. And when he climbed up the ladders, which she insisted on holding, she felt a burning desire for a close-up of what the vulgar, according to the addendum to the current Dictionary of Slang, still called on both sides of the Atlantic his "Builders' Crack".

In the 1990s people tucked their shirts or blouses into their trousers or skirts; brick layers did not. The combination of the Wolf Whistle and a variety of hand signals were a turn-on for some sorts of young women, though not for her. She thought that builders were at their best when they stooped and rhythmically broke the gritty cement into a mess which resembled porridge in its consistency. It was when they were bending, dignified by labour, that that most intimate aspect of their anatomy appeared. She also loved the thought of a labourer's rough hands. Arthur's hands were feminine. He daily used moisturiser.

I DO NOT SPOT ANY CULTURAL PROBLEMS HERE. BUT BE CAREFUL. SHE SEEMS A NORMAL ENOUGH 40-PLUS, RADICAL YORKSHIRE WOMAN. NOTHING MUCH HAS HAPPENED.

Akbar stepped onto the ladder carrying the sixth and seventh box. After a couple of steps, she moved forward and held its sides. His body passed between her and the ladder and at that point his builders' cleft and the top of a pair of Kelvin Klein boxer shorts appeared. She had an inclination to kiss the emerging skin but decided not to. Young Mr Akhbar might, or might not, have liked it.

Do you think this is the start of a novel?

I SHOULDN'T THINK SO. END END END.

When Fat Ruled the World

Helen Shay

LEKA THE LUSCIOUS HAD LOST by one dress size.
A whole world of personally-tailored twenty-second-
century comfort-eating could not put that right.

The Sponsorettes wheeled her onto the stage into the
muted spotlight reserved for second place. Leka forced her
lips to widen as if to smile, baring her sugar-rotted teeth and
listening to the stilted applause, beneath which the audience
whispered: "Second is failure".

One thing even worse remained. Leka tensed herself
for the announcement.

"And in first place – Drevina the Delectable!"

Cheers erupted, as the bearers carried the dais on
which the queen of the hour spread out her fleshly folds of
glory.

"The Planet's Next Top Model!"

Shrieks and wolf whistles sang around as Drevina
alighted, then waddled before them in an electric blue PVC
tent dress. In spite of her pique, Leka had to admit that
Drevina cut a fine figure. Her breasts looped down like
inverted camel humps over her stomach, orchestrating its
wobble in a way that had set all four judges drooling. Leka's
own folds could match those; but when it came to buttocks,
Drevina had (almost literally) knocked them dead. Each
breezy sway of her hips had taken a full minute to subside and
her final fat-catwalk had clinched the title. The viewers'
votes had flooded in.

"I'd like to thank those who helped me to this great
honour – my pastry chef, my chocolatier and of course my
personal nurturer..." droned Drevina.

159

Leka looked across to her own nurturer. Reynor's dark eyes were fixed upon her from the wings. "I told you so," they said, "That cream pint you wouldn't drink, that Turkish delight you wouldn't finish, that...." Leka could imagine the boy's secret reproaches. He'd served her so well – nine meals a day – in the run-up to the competition. Back in the Select Quarters, he'd groomed her morning and night, massaging molecular-matched anti-fungal oils into her ever-deepening creases, applying mask-film foundation fillers to her face and chins, and web-tonging ringlets into her floppy fair hair to enhance the rotundity of her features.

"This is *the* Beauty Contest," was his mantra. "The ones chosen for this epitomise the new aesthetic, which will lead us out of post-third world war disillusion. The State applauds your dedication to inertia, your forbearance from activity, your devotion to size – because it matters. It is my honour to serve so resplendent a mistress, who ranks amongst the best aspirational role-models."

Leka could see how Reynor had got his job. So politically-correct and a vegan to boot. The Mediatrollers were always wary of allowing meat-eaters too near their prize girls. Perhaps they feared they'd steal some of the food and upset the carefully balanced program of limitless calories; or worse still, turn out to be far too red-blooded amongst so much tempting flesh. Vegans were seen as the safe option – the eunuchs of the epicurean harem housed within the Select Quarter. For the girls of course must remain virgins.

Whereas a few centuries ago, "meek and mild" had been the feminine ideal, now it was "fat and pure". Besides, they ran a different program for those fit-to-mate and reproduce, equally carefully controlled and with babies removed at birth for genetic grading. But who would want to be segregated to that messy business, suffering sex and such like, when they could instead live a life of eating – and eating and eating?

That's what Reynor had said anyway, his brown eyes shifting slightly as he gazed into hers, as she fed. Leka wondered about him sometimes. His face with its *café latte* hue might be pleasant enough, if only it were not so thin with its protruding cheekbones and lack of any hint of a double chin. Worse still, he had muscles. Leka knew she must make some allowance for his having to carry her to and from her chair, but did he really have to develop them on his legs and chest as well as arms? *Mr No-Boundary Universe* he would never be. Those who competed for that title were superheroes of the overhang.

But now that Drevina had beaten her, Leka would never meet *her* Mr Universe. What would become of her now? Would she suddenly disappear like those other girls who'd lost before? There were rumours of "accidental" overdoses of metabolism suppressants. After all, it had always been a common phenomenon that some girls could never quite balance eating and death. Some would just reach tipping point and something inside would implode. But there were other rumours too – of convenient new careers at the hospitality houses. *Brothels more like*, thought Leka. Once maidenhead was auctioned and lost, it was all downhill. No-one, even in this advanced and modern PC society, wanted a fat old slapper.

"... and my suckling pig-turner, and last but by no means least, my goose-fat supplier."

Drevina was now punctuating her speech with what she seemed to regard as a tasteful striptease, allowing the awe-struck audience gradual glimpses of her squidgiest bits. The electric blue PVC had given way to a red fishnet body stocking beneath. This was Drevina in full splendour. Leka could only watch and weep.

Just for a moment, Leka wondered if she should after all have accepted Siscar's offer. Reynor would never have approved, she knew. "Beware, mistress! Illicit feeders are the scum of our advanced society," he'd proclaimed. Yet Leka had heard they were a great way to get fat. Maybe even fatter than Drevina. But then she recalled Siscar's long, cold fingers, which he had run over her mouth, as he'd offered himself to her as her "special nourisher". Leka shivered at the memory and knew Reynor was right.

Back in her assigned boudoir, Leka saw the discreet disappointment in Reynor's demeanour as he peeled off her sweat-sodden white ballgown.

"Should I have worn PVC and fishnet too, then?" she ventured. He smiled but remained silent. "Okay, you think I should have eaten more, don't you?"

"It's not the amount you ate, Mistress.'

"What? Are ye olde reconstituted fish and chips with scraps too healthy and uncalorific these days?" Leka snapped.

"It's not what you ate or didn't eat. It's what you didn't *digest*."

Leka felt her face flush with heat and anger. Or was it heat and shame? How dare he, a mere vegan, challenge her with that! Her fist lashed him in the chest, knocking him to the ground. She might be too fat to walk, but she was still heavy enough to pack a punch.

"I heard. In the latrinal. All those times," he wheezed, "Retching and retching."

"How dare you accuse me of such a thing? Bulimia is a criminal offence."

"I know. And I know you. You don't want this. You want to spew it out – every taste."

Leka felt the tears pour their fire onto her already burning cheeks. "Reynor, don't ..."

"Tell the truth? You don't want this. You never did."

Now it was she who was silent.

"Come away, Leka. Leave this madness, this sick place."

Leka laughed. "What would you suggest? That I go to the Dogs? Does coming second mean that's all I'm fit for?"

Reynor rose, staring at her, then taking her hand. "It's not what they say. The Dogs and all that. It's just different. Wild. Free."

Leka laughed again, but her hand remained in his. "You're the one who's mad."

"No, Leka. I can show you. It's not what they say. Out there!"

Leka shrank from him. "Just go. I need to sleep."

She slumped on the bed as he slammed the door. "He'll be back," she consoled herself. "...and he'll be sorry." She *was* his mistress after all.

IN THE DARK came the touch. Soft at first, stroking away the covers and then slowly along her leg – ankle to knee, thigh to groin. Leka stirred.

"Reynor,' she murmured.

"Darling," whispered back the dark. The touch continued, deeper and insistent, beginning to hurt.

"Oh, luscious indeed!" The voice was heavy now, punctuated by panting breath. Leka fumbled for her bedside illuminator, then blinked through the sudden light.

"Siscar!"

"Yes, it is I, your *servilest* servant. Here to offer solace in your chagrin."

"Solace?"

"You were robbed. The judges were blind to your infinite beauty, and as for the people – peasants blind to your largess of flesh and soul, your ..."

"How did you get in here, Siscar, without the sitters stopping you?"

163

"Oh, sitters too have their cravings. Not as sophisticated as you delicious girls, but a little coinage does the trick."

"Trick?"

"Lovely Leka. You mustn't think of that. So what if I did give ... *special coaching* to dreadful Drevina? After you refused me, can you really blame me? But it was always you I wanted."

Leka's mind finally emerged from the hangover of sleep to the sobering revelation that this was not a dream, only her worst nightmare come true. Siscar, in all his poison, was actually here.

"Are you saying you fed Drevina?"

"Oh, come, Leka. The relationship between feeder and feedee goes beyond food, as you can now discover – and taste – for yourself."

"I demand a replay! The contest is void!"

Siscar giggled. "Silly little girl. Solace I said, and solace I offer. Come now. Look what I've brought for you! Caviar-dipped chicken nuggets. A big mac mega-decker with starter, main and dessert tiered into one. Oh, please, bite it, my darling."

"I'll bite *you*!"

"Okay, that's nice too. But first, my sweeting, suck on this."

Siscar thrust towards her mouth. She felt something hard and boney prise her teeth apart, as a sickly liquid goo dribbled onto her tongue. Leka strained to lift her knee and kicked him away. He gazed up at her from the floor, trembling from physical and emotional pain, still holding up the thumb he had pressed upon her. Brown globules dripped from it onto the rush-matting floor.

"This was the best sticky toffee sauce in the Reformed World," he said incredulously, "You refuse that and me?"

"I wouldn't lick your thumb if it were the last toffee sauce on the planet! Crawl back to your hole and die!"

Siscar giggled again. "I'll have you drenched in it and crawling to me for tit-bits. Second is failure. You're out, Leka the Luscious, and I've already bought a bond over you from the Sponsors. You're mine now, to force-feed as I choose."

Leka retaliated with the only weapon she had, her weight. She rolled off the bed, knocking Siscar to the ground, then spread herself over him until his squealing stopped. "How's that for an easy lay then, Siscar? Leg-over enough for you?"

But suddenly the smell hit her. The mix of chicken nuggets, burger, toffee sauce and Siscar's excretion, now that fear of her had hit him along with her bulk, became too much. She barfed. And as she did so, it seemed that all her life vomited before her – the endless eating, the constant battle to get fat, the weigh-ins that never tipped the scales enough, *Weightpilers* and their stupid points system, the "Big is beautiful but bigger is better" slogan – right down to now, this final violation. He'd wanted only to foist food upon her, but still she felt defiled. She could take no more.

Leka was still sitting on the unconscious Siscar, now covered in regurgitated supper, when Reynor returned. "What...!"

"Get me out of here, I'm a failed obesity goddess," Leka sobbed, "Maybe I *am* only fit for the Dogs. Take me away, like you said!"

EVEN WITH the wheelchair, they sneaked passed the sitters easily, as most of them had snuck off early to spend Siscar's bribes. Getting out of the prize compound proved harder, but Reynor told the gaters that his charge had an urgent appointment with the toe-cutter.

"Ingrowing. You know how it is, and she can't reach them herself. I've refused to do it. Pedicures are not in my job description."

The guards had simply nodded, looking Leka up and down with undisguised politically-correct lust.

It was dark when they reached the outpost. Leka was sleeping in the chair, when Reynor roused her. "You're snoring too loud. You'll alert the sentries. Besides, you'll have to get out now."

Leka looked at him. "You mean … walk?"

"I think they'd notice me pushing a wheelchair over the border."

"But … walk? All those soldiers?"

"Could you manage a crawl? Just a slow one?"

The Great Escape, this clearly was not. Reynor tipped her out by a clump of bushes, in which he then hid the chair. "Now we wait for dawn," he said.

"Why? Surely darkness gives more cover?"

"Because that's when the sentry at this guardpoint takes time out for his pipe.'

"Pipe? No-one's allowed to smoke in any form since that edict against appetite suppressants."

Reynor smirked. "You'll find life is not so… regulated outside the compound."

Leka snuggled down beside him to wait, wondering what exactly was a *not so regulated* life. But neither the relaxation nor the speculation lasted for long.

"Leka, come on!" he ordered for the tenth time, once they had got past and out of range of the sentry station.

Leka swore back once more. Reynor lifted her to her feet and pushed her on. But yet again, she stumbled. There was hardly anything to stumble over in this barren terrain but Leka's feet seemed to manage it. On the horizon, the outline of a huge rock loomed. The sun shone down upon them, making them feel more exposed and teasing Leka's pale skin into a shade of pink grapefruit.

"I get rosacea, you know."

"So? Maybe you'd like to lie down a while, Leka. I'll call out some coolies and see if they might have an outsize sedan handy to carry you in."

Leka stared into his dark eyes, which didn't need to squint in the sunlight like her own watery blue. She tried to recall the exact moment in the last few hours when the power had switched in their relationship. Just when had he stopped calling her *mistress*? And what was she now to him? Certainly not mistress in *any* form. Too many questions when she felt so exhausted! Yet how had he known about the sentry's break? Why had he led her here? Siscar had left her no choice but to go. Becoming bondslave to him was not just a fate worse than death, it would be a form of death with hell and all the trimmings. But turning instinctively to the one who had nurtured her, being led out here in the sun that burnt her flesh, felt literally from frying pan to fire. She sank to her knees, her thighs expanding like a pair of fleshy wings.

Reynor tutted. "You know what, Leka? Why don't you just have a nice sleep here, until the vultures gather?"

Leka placed her head in her hands. She would not let him see her cry.

"Yes, close your eyes. Rest a while."

Leka heard something stir. Behind? Or was it above? Something stealing upon her. But then it turned into nothing. There was only the pain and the fall into black.

THE FIRST THING she heard on waking was the howling. So that was it then. She'd finally gone to the Dogs. Her eyes adjusted to the dark, then wished they had not. The usual "home" scenario was gone. No warm bed with jars of boiled sweets on the dressing table and Reynor greeting her with a dozen butter croissants. Instead there was this dank atmosphere and nothing but stone. The only decor seemed to be moss and green fungus. The only common factor that remained was Reynor, only without a tray. "Welcome to cave life," he said.

Suddenly a gurgling roar erupted about them. Leka tensed, then blushed, realising that it was her stomach. Its withdrawal from an habitual meal on the hour, every hour, had made it thunder with deprivation.

"Hey, I *have* been feeding you," protested Reynor, "milk and porridge. Did you realise you can eat in your sleep? Automatic reflex by now."

Just then more howling echoed around them, drowning out even Leka's stomach.

"I don't need to ask where you brought me. It's to them!" she shouted, "You're an infiltrator, aren't you, Reynor? A traitor to Civilisation! All planned. The get-away, the sentry."

"Even the coolies with the extra large sedan to get you here. Well, more of mobile hammock – king-size. Sorry they had to knock you out first, but I knew your legs would never make it any further under all the rest of you."

Leka winced at his pejorative tone. She had never before been criticised for her bulk. Heavy was beautiful. Everyone knew that. But in *his* eyes she saw only disgust. That sickened her more than even Siscar and his toffee-drenched thumb. It scared her too. All the rules had changed. "What are you going to do with me?"

"Don't worry, you'll be looked after. The Dogs aren't all you've been told. We're not savages, we're free." As if to underline – or undermine – his point, the howling outside repeated even more loudly. "They just do that, Leka. Sort of a custom to welcome the new moon."

"So *many* welcomes round here, then."

Reynor looked at her, then stroked her tangled hair. "You'll meet Wulf soon. Then you'll understand." His tone was soft now but she still perceived contempt in his eyes. He passed her more milk and porridge but, for the first time, left her to eat alone. She wanted to leave it untouched, a stoic attempt at dignity, but her stomach volcanoed its rumbling again and she crammed it down.

Hours later, Reynor returned.

"Is this my take-me-to-your-leader moment?" she quipped. "Wulf – your original caveman warrior? Bear skins and hair everywhere, plus of course the wolf's head headdress?"

"We're all cavemen in the end. Maybe if we'd all eaten like them, you'd never have got to be such a mess."

Leka was about to throw the porridge in his face, but remembered that hunger had triumphed over dignity. Instead she followed him out of the cave mouth. Rain fell from the dull, grey-cloud sky. She could feel the staring eyes upon her from those who sheltered in the caves. She shivered, then shrieked as something gnawed at her ankles.

"Jep, no!" commanded Reynor.

Leka stared down at the skinny, bedraggled hound, now whining as Reynor slapped its nose. "Yes, we do have dogs. But we live like men."

"And what of the women?"

"Oh, you'll learn all about the women."

He led her into a tunnel formed in the rock face, lighting a lantern to show the way. She was soon out of breath in the struggle to keep pace. Suddenly the path opened into a large cavern, thronged with people, who made the dog look fat and well-groomed. They seemed to be chanting – or more humming – one monotone note, blatantly off-key. So this is the full welcome, thought Leka. But then came silence. Before her stood a tall, slim woman dressed in white.

"I am Wulf," said the woman, "We are glad you are here."

Her embrace caught Leka off-guard, especially as it concluded with a long kiss on the lips. Wulf smelt of musk and autumn. As they pulled apart, the flat hum resumed to reach new heights of atonality. Wulf smiled. Leka could not resist returning this.

Wulf took her arm and led her to an ante-chamber, away from the throng. It was lit by candles and housed a long table, at which sat several girls dressed in black, who rose and saluted as Wulf entered to take her place at the head. She gestured Leka to sit beside her. It seemed strange to eat a formal meal without Reynor. However, Leka need not have worried, as *eat* felt like a euphemism. The meal which ensued was sugar-rush-free and for her devoid of substance. Most of it was green.

"Herbs," Wulf explained, as they chomped through heaps of leaves. Dessert comprised a few berries, washed down with some form of fiery distilled liquid. The alcohol shot to Leka's head, with so few calories to offer a barrier. Back in the compound, Reynor would have censured her for drinking. She now drank deeper at the thought.

"... so now you see what freedom is," extolled Wulf, "Away from when fat ruled the world. Away from those who swell women up like cattle, then parade them for the gratification of a populace raised to watch and grin, to eat themselves into sloth – until the fat oozes between the brain cells and stops all connections.'

Lacking much knowledge of neurology, Leka chose simply to nod. In fact, it seemed that the meal for her had consisted much of "munch and nod", punctuated of course by more fire-water. The more she munched, nodded and drank, the more Wulf seemed exactly right. Her past life had been one of insane exploitation, lived out in that post-tertiary war of pretend plenty, where competitive weight gain and compulsive eating distracted the people from looking beyond themselves – from asking too many questions. Far better to

170

be here, free and wild. Far better to munch and nod, and drink.

"Cheers!" Reynor leant across the table and clinked her goblet with his. *When had he joined them?* she wondered. He looked different here, less regimented. He wore leather breeches and waistcoat, showing off those awful muscles. Only they didn't look quite so bad in this light. In fact, all those at the table looked pretty good, albeit emaciated. That's what dandelion leaves and blackberries did for you in the end. *But what the hell!*

"To dandesleans and berries black!" declared Leka, sloshing her drink over the table. Wulf laughed and the others took their cue to do so also.

"You know these girls were once like you?" whispered Wulf in Leka's ear, licking the lobe as she did so. "Runners-up who fled the compound – with our help. We get them in the end. Absorb them one way or another.'

The lick became a bite. Leka winced, looking up to see Reynor staring at her.

"She doesn't need a minder now, Reynor. You can go back to the men now."

THE REST of the night seemed lost to Leka somewhere in her hangover the next morning. She woke, back in her allotted cave, cold and aching the following midday, but anaesthetised by her own bewilderment. That word itself pulsated in her throbbing head: *be-wilder-ment*. Perhaps that's where she was now, in a land of "be wilder". Trouble was, "wild" seemed to mean very hungry.

But soon the other girls came to rescue her with yet more berries. Then they washed her with spring water and dressed her in a grey tunic. "You will progress to black," they told her, "if Wulf decides – as your life unfolds."

As the weeks passed, the unfolding seemed to apply more to Leka's skin. The green diet took its toll on the carefully cultivated years of fat. At least that helped her mobility, especially as the women insisted she joined their regime of manual work, tending livestock and gathering pickings from the land. The men were left to train for the hunting trips, come the full moon, and on which – preluded by extra howling – so much hope was placed. Maybe this time, out in that empty landscape they would find something on which to prey. But so often they returned with nothing.

"The Goddess will grace us next time," said Wulf. Then she would gather the women and lead them deep into the rock to perform the untold rites. Leka still dressed in grey and was not allowed to join.

Reynor came to her one day, as she waited outside for the women to return. "You look…"

"Thin?"

"Well, *I'm* glad."

"Back in the Civilised World you'd be arrested for such a comment. Echoes of the old world – anorexic models snorting coke so as not to eat. Exploitation comes in all sizes. I should know."

"Which size will you choose, Leka?"

"The one that keeps me alive."

Reynor seized her hand. "I shouldn't have brought you here. Forgive me."

"Oh, it's fine. I can even walk quite well now. And let's face it. Whatever they told us back there, who'd really drool over me, except maybe a cannibal?"

Reynor laughed, then looked over his shoulder and squeezed her hand tight. "Don't let them see you bleed, Leka."

A mix of humming and howling enfolded them, as Wulf and her women re-emerged. Their faces were painted now, daubed with the red paste they'd made from holly berries, next to which their white teeth gleamed.

"DON'T LET THEM see you bleed!"

The words ran through Leka's dreams for several nights, but it was not until the waning that she found herself alone with him again. It seemed that the wilderness had its own code of segregation, enforced by its implicit matriarchy. They met by chance when Jep – whose instant love-hate attraction to her had never subsided – decided to snivel round her legs once more.

"I'm sorry about this," said Reynor, "He's a bad dog – and rubbish in the full moon hunt. Not the hound I wanted, but they've stuck me with him."

"Do they time everything by the moon here?"

"Just about. It's a woman thing, isn't it?"

"What did you mean by *bleed*? Another woman thing?"

He did not answer. Not even when they went into her cave, not even on the hard stone shelf that formed her bed, not even after the mating, when her cries – hidden under the howling outside – were over, not even when they parted and whispered their farewells.

"Well, now I can never go back," she said, "Neither fat nor pure."

SO FAR they had not been discovered – except occasionally by Jep, who kept his snarls to himself. Nights of subterfuge and passion waxed and waned to their own rhythm. The cave seemed not so made of stone after all, its cold walls refreshing in the heat. Until...

"It's time to stop," she said one night.

"Try to stop me."

"Wulf has told me to live with the other women in the main cave from now on."

"No!"

"At least now I've a chance to pass from grey to black."

173

"Or white."

"Only Wulf wears white."

"Not always." He fell silent for a moment. "You mustn't go in there. You mustn't live with them."

"We can still try to meet. The woods maybe."

"You mustn't live with them, Leka. They'll see you bleed."

"Is this some twisted jealousy?"

"You'll live with the other women. They'll wait for you to bleed with them. Once you're in sync at the new moon, they'll take that for the sign. Then you'll be dressed in white. You'll be the next. They need it for the hunt. It's become so futile again. Bad moons."

"Seems to me that *you're* the lunatic, Reynor."

"But once they see you bleed ..."

Leka laughed. "Look, don't worry, I've no interest in the women. We can still meet. And anyway, I may not bleed at all, it seems."

Reynor's brow furrowed, as he stared at her in question.

"Not for two months now. Ever since... I might even get to be *fat* again."

Reynor remained silent, then seized her by the shoulders. "Leka, you mustn't let them find out."

"Look, I won't say it's you. I won't confess."

"You won't have to. Don't you know only Wulf is allowed to conceive? And she says we have too many mouths to feed for now. Until the hunt improves – by the grace of the goddess." Reynor spat at the floor. "You're here to ensure that, Leka. As the next sacrifice."

"What? But it was you who brought me here. You knew."

"No! She doesn't use all the girls we get. You've seen them. Some she keeps as her acolytes. The ones who make it to wear black. I didn't know until after I brought you

174

that she'd definitely... She says we need meat. The hunts have been so bad."

"You brought me here ... for meat!"

"She doesn't always do that, I told you."

"You brought me here for m..."

"*Me*! I asked you to leave with me, remember? Not that I'd planned it, or wanted it."

"Thanks."

"Leka, I was meant to recruit one of the Select. Get taken on as a nurturer. I got you."

"How terrible for you!"

"I mean, it's just how it turned out. And it was no problem until ... Well, not even when I got to know you."

"To know me is not to..."

"Until I really knew you. Mad, I know. It was sort of love at first vomit, I suppose. As soon as I saw that really you rejected all that, wanted to hurl it out... Then I hoped if I got you here, she wouldn't choose you for white, the blood at the full moon, the feast and all that. I know it's horrible, but she has such power. We've got to get away. Beyond the civilised and the wild. We've got to get away. Especially now."

Leka clasped her hands upon her abdomen. "Yes, especially now."

THE MOON WAS full but clouded on the night they chose. The women were howling as usual, and the men were setting off for the hunt, as the couple stole their way down from the rock. Leka did not stumble any more. Hardly cat-like as yet, but no longer the porpoise out of water she once was. Reynor's agility was handicapped only by the provisions and knife he bore, as they headed for the trees below. Once they crossed the stream, their scent would be lost to the dogs, should their escape be discovered.

But in the end, it was a dog that betrayed them. Not until he charged upon Leka did they know Jep was following.

Reynor struck him but that only intensified his barks. Leka fought against the instinct to scream, as the dog's incisors pierced her arm. Reynor fell upon it with his knife, its blood mingling with his own as they fought. From above they heard the women shrieking out and calling the men back. Soon they would spot where the escapers were.

"Go, Leka!" shouted Reynor.

"I won't leave you."

"You must!"

The dog clung to life, pinning him down and tearing at his throat. The deeper the knife dug into its hide, the more ferocious was its bite. By the time it finally died, as Leka kicked it away, Reynor said only one more word.

"Go!"

BY DAWN Leka had reached the forest, making her way through mud and marsh, despite visibility impaired by tears. She had crossed over the stream, and the noise of the hunters in pursuit had long since faded. But she would not stop. Not now. She thought of the one she had lost and the one she carried within her. Her body braced itself against the wind. She looked ahead into the unknown wasteland where she must find a new life. And then, for the first time in her life, she ran – and ran, and ran.

The Authors

Philip Andrews was born in Wakefield and spent his early years in the nearby mining town of Normanton. He is a journalist, novelist and lecturer. He has worked for regional and national newspapers (winning a number of awards, including that of Yorkshire Sports Journalist of the Year three times), radio and television (latterly as an on-screen reporter for Leeds-based ITV news programme *Calendar*). His novels *Own Goals* and *Goodnight Vienna* are published by Hodder and Stoughton. His textbook *Sports Journalism, a Practical Guide* (Sage), is used in universities around the world and has been translated into many languages. He currently lectures in journalism at Sheffield Hallam University.

Sue Featherstone is a former journalist and public relations practitioner turned academic. She moved to Yorkshire aged nine. Her writing career started in local newspapers before switching to PR. She completed a degree in English Literature as a mature student and subsequently moved into higher education, teaching journalism at Sheffield Hallam University. At the beginning of 2017, Sue left Sheffield Hallam to focus on her writing. Together with her writing partner Susan Pape, she has written two journalism text books – *Newspaper Journalism: A Practical Introduction*; and *Feature Writing: A Practical Introduction*. Their first novel, *A Falling Friend*, was published by Lakewater Press in 2016; and a sequel, provisionally titled *Calls Herself a Friend*, will follow later this year. They now write about books at https://bookloversbooklist. com/
Sue is on twitter @SueF_Writer

Neil Fieldhouse is an award-winning journalist who has written extensively for newspapers, radio and television. He was born in a mining village near Wakefield and worked for regional newspapers in Yorkshire before moving to Whitby to run a guest house with his journalist wife Kate. He now lives in a village sandwiched between the North York Moors and the North Sea. His first novel *Silent Night* was published to acclaim and his second *The Painter of Souls* is due out in 2018. His English teacher wisely advised the only way he would make money from typewriters was to charge people for repairing them.

Diane Galloway was born in the Yorkshire village of Askern, famous for its coal. Her father was a clerk for the colliery, her mother a war evacuee from Hull. She attended local schools and gained a scholarship to Don Valley High, leaving with an Art degree. She worked behind the counter of the local Chemist; an ideal place to observe the eccentricities of Yorkshire folk. She married a Scotsman and moved to Scotland, eventually returning to Yorkshire where her husband began work at South Kirkby colliery. Together they raised a family of one son and two daughters in the town of Hemsworth and retired to a cottage in the small village of Womersley. Now a widow, Diane enjoys spending time with her family and being creative.

Shree Ganguly lived in India as a child. She came to Yorkshire in 2009 and has been inspired by the Yorkshire landscape ever since, and the curious juxtaposition of cultures that she has been exposed to. This is her first short story to be published. She is currently working on a novel that explores the theme of power and freedom.

Colin Hollis was born in the small mining town of Featherstone, and lived there until moving to Sheffield to study for a physics degree. After a short while working in science, he became a teacher, living and working in Wakefield. He then wrote and published the fantasy novel he'd always wanted to: *Herbmaster of Tarodash*. A second novel, a crime story set somewhere in the Wakefield to Pontefract area, is almost ready for publication, as is a book of short stories. When not writing, he spends his time running, reading, woodworking, and watching Yorkshire play cricket.

Linda Jones was born in Newport, South Wales. Working in the field of Mental Health, she lived and worked in many parts of the country, finally settling with her family in Ackworth, West Yorkshire, over 18 years ago. Illness meant a drastic career change and it was then she finally found the courage to put pen to paper. Her first children's novel *A Fistful of Feathers* was published by independent publishing house The Writing Hall in 2016. The second in the series is due for release soon. *Points of Convergence* is Linda's second adult short story to be published.

Brian Lewis is a publisher who has published over 150 books. In 1992 he won the Raymond Williams prize for Community Publishing and has an Honorary Doctorate from Sheffield Hallam for services to the arts and community. A pragmatist, he likes challenging himself – and in 2015 he wrote three novels in a year to learn the craft. This experimental story reflects his interest and the problems of self-criticism.

Susan McCartney lives in Castleford. She was born in Leeds but left in 1968 to join the WRAF. She returned to Yorkshire in 1992 to take up a job in Pontefract as a teacher. Susan is a member of several writing groups and has seen her stories displayed, recorded, and published. As part of the Bus Pass People group, Susan went to Stratford to perform in a version of *King Lear* set in Wakefield. This trip gave her the first opportunity to do an open mic session. Since that time, she has written and performed several of her poems. Her next challenge is to master the ukulele.

Helen Shay is from Yorkshire, growing up in West Leeds and now living in North Yorkshire. She writes short stories, drama and poetry (which she also performs) with a recent collection *Scop,* available on http://nettlebooks.weebly.com/ She runs a Spoken Word event *Poems, Prose and Pints,* in Harrogate every third Wednesday of the month. Helen currently serves on the Society of Authors' Poetry and Spoken Word Group Committee.

Joan Thornton has compiled and edited many community books, has been involved in a number of arts, publishing and creative writing projects in Yorkshire, and has had a number of short stories published and broadcast. She has had a varied and well-travelled career and draws on these experiences in her writing, but growing up in South Yorkshire in the fifties and sixties has been a rich and endless source of inspiration. She now divides her time between France and York and spends more time in her garden and walking than she does writing. She is however helping to produce a publication about the local history and footpaths of the Brittany coastline, and teaches English to mature French students. She is saving her remaining fund of stories until she can no longer abseil and wind surf, when she will retreat to her attic and write best sellers to supplement her pension and home-grown radish crop.

Steven B. Williams is a tea-swilling, curly-haired writer and poet from West Yorkshire. When not working on dark fantasy, he can be found scribbling about queer rights and mental health. His debut novel *Heartsnare* was published by Lethe Press in October 2016 to critical praise, and he is earning a name for himself as a spoken word poet, elevating the voice of the LGBTQIA community. Connect with him on Facebook, Instagram, Twitter and across social media by searching "@stevenbwriting".

John Winter can only be said to have qualified as a Yorkshire writer through nearly 30 years experience as a journalist at the *Sheffield Star*. He was, in fact, born in the Isle of Wight, where his novel *Heaven Scent* is based, pure fiction of course. "I can understand how satisfied Yorkshire folk are of their county, for it has everything: gritty cities, beautiful countryside and coast, and fanatically proud citizens," he says. " I can understand the emotional ties that bind Yorkshire folk to their place of birth, and was delighted to be asked to take part in this celebration of Yorkshire writers."

Michael Yates, who lives in Wakefield, was reporter and later film critic with the *Sheffield Star*. He taught playwriting at Harrogate Theatre and creative writing for the WEA. He has published short stories in anthologies and magazines and won story prizes from the Jersey Arts Centre, the Armagh Writers Festival, the Wolds Words Festival and the Writers & Artists Yearbook. He has had a dozen plays performed in the north of England – including Leeds, Bradford, Liverpool and Manchester – winning an award at the Sheffield One-Act Play Festival. And he has been Poet in Residence in Whitby, Wakefield Cathedral and Wakefield Hospitals.

Fiction in Nettle Books

Pomfret
Editor: Brian Lewis

Ten stories about historical Yorkshire town Pontefract by Yorkshire writers including Colin Hollis, Howard Frost, Linda Jones, Robin Gledhill, Ann Rhodes, Walter Storey, John A Goodrich and Susan McCartney.
ISBN: 978-0-9561513-8-4   **£8**

Heaven Scent
John Winter

A comic novel set in the swinging sixties. Charlie wanted to be part of the sexual revolution but it passed him by. Now working on a seaside weekly paper, he has something to take his minds off summers of love. The sleepy resort is rocked by mystery explosions. Is it the Isle of Wight Republican Army?
ISBN:978-0-9561513-6-0   **£10**

Homer's ODC
Michael Yates

Raymond wishes he'd gone to Uni. But his father wants him in the family business. And his father is a gangster. Barry wants to be a poet. But he's also – in his own words – a user of the mental health services. A shot rings out. It's the shot that brings Ray and Barry together and sets off a sequence of violent events that ends in grim murder and even grimmer poetry.
ISBN:978-0-9561513-7-7   **£10**

#0120 - 290517 - C0 - 210/148/10 - PB - DID1852079